### *"I'm not getting dressed with you sitting here."*

"Go down to the lobby and wait for me," Shane instructed. She wondered how many women would dare to talk this way to him.

"The lobby?" Nick asked, feigning horror. "Madam, do you realize what awaits me down there?"

"What?" she asked, playing along.

"Why, there might be legions of my fans downstairs by now," he said, still using dialogue that might have sprung out of one of his costume dramas.

Shane sighed. "If you're swept away, I'll understand. I'll find you. Never fear."

"That's not the problem."

"Then what is?" she asked impatiently. He was the problem, she thought, and smiled grimly at him.

"Why, they might just surround me and tear off all my clothes. It's been known to happen, you know. You wouldn't want to go anywhere with me naked, would you?" The grin spread, covering every handsome inch of his face. "Or would you?" he asked, rakishly cocking his head.

## WHAT ARE *LOVESWEPT* ROMANCES?

They are stories of true romance and touching emotion. We believe those two very important ingredients are constants in our highly sensual and very believable stories in the *LOVESWEPT* line. Our goal is to give you, the reader, stories of consistently high quality that may sometimes make you laugh, sometimes make you cry, but are always fresh and creative and contain many delightful surprises within their pages.

Most romance fans read an enormous number of books. Those they truly love, they keep. Others may be traded with friends and soon forgotten. We hope that each *LOVESWEPT* romance will be a treasure—a "keeper." We will always try to publish

*LOVE STORIES YOU'LL NEVER FORGET*
*BY AUTHORS YOU'LL ALWAYS REMEMBER*

The Editors

**LOVESWEPT · 37**

# Marie Michael

# Irresistible Forces

BANTAM BOOKS · TORONTO · NEW YORK · LONDON · SYDNEY

IRRESISTIBLE FORCES

*A Bantam Book / March 1984*

*LOVESWEPT and the wave device are trademarks of*
*Bantam Books, Inc.*

ISBN 0-553-21641-4

*Published simultaneously in the United States and Canada*

Bantam Books are published by Bantam Books, Inc. Its trademark,
consisting of the words "Bantam Books" and the portrayal of a
rooster, is Registered in U.S. Patent and Trademark Office and in
other countries. Marca Registrada. Bantam Books, Inc., 666 Fifth
Avenue, New York, New York 10103.

PRINTED IN THE UNITED STATES OF AMERICA

O    0 9 8 7 6 5 4 3 2 1

*This book is dedicated to*
*C. N.,*
*with gratitude*
*for her faith*
*in me*

# One

The thready voice of Theodore Banks, editor-in-chief of *Rendezvous*, piped through the smoke-filled air in the ash-paneled conference room. Shane McCallister's deep blue eyes never left the gaunt face of the tall man at the head of the table as he gave out assignments for the next issue of the magazine. And then, suddenly, Shane went rigid with shock, her expectations crumbling, her well-ordered plans flying all over the place like smashed smithereens.

"Anderson, I've chosen you for the key interview." A half smile slashed across Banks's face as he glanced at Shane before quickly redirecting his gaze to Anderson. "With the President," he added—for unnecessary emphasis, Shane thought. "There'll be a secret service man waiting to meet you at National Airport. He'll inform you of all the dos and don'ts—see if you can get around them."

Bill Anderson, a heavyset man in his fifties, looked surprised at the plum assignment. Well, more than surprised, really. He looked stunned. Everyone had been sure Shane had the interview in the bag.

So had Shane.

"And as for you, McCallister," Banks said, his piercing eyes pinning her once more, "I want a story on Nick Rutledge."

"The movie star?" Shane asked, shock making her voice quaver and her eyebrows rise perilously close to her hairline. This was unbelievable. The kinds of interviews the magazine usually ran were concerned with the movers and shakers of the world. Shane hardly thought that Hollywood—and Nick Rutledge, especially—was an appropriate subject for a classy magazine like *Rendezvous*.

"That 'movie star' is single-handedly responsible for bringing romance back into the movies." Banks steepled his fingers, then looked at Shane over the pyramid they made. "He's become a legend after only five years. He's the stuff that Valentino and Gable were made of. The readers," he pronounced with imperial authority, "will be interested in learning about him. And," he added, an expression touched with whimsy flitting across his face, "this needs a 'woman's touch.' " His satisfaction with that last comment was only too obvious.

Shane struggled to keep the bitterness from showing—and lost the battle. How she hated his patronizing her this way! "Then why don't you give the assignment to Anderson?" she asked, her voice very low, yet firm with anger. "His prose is much more flowery than mine."

"McCallister," Banks said in a slow, threatening roar before growing snappish. "I make the decisions around here."

"Then, you've made a wrong one," Shane insisted, rising. Her fingers fanned out on the oak table as she leaned forward, her five-foot two-inch frame challenging him the way a mongoose challenges a cobra. "That assignment was mine, and you know it! As a senior writer—"

"You are senior writer only if I say so, young woman. And I do not say so." Banks's thin eyebrows were drawn into one straight, angry line across his pale forehead.

"Why not?" Shane demanded.

Everyone else in the conference room had grown still with apprehension over this virtually unprecedented confrontation.

A nasty smile now creased the sharp features of Shane's editor-in-chief. "Because, McCallister, unlike the old editor, who was a soft touch, I do not believe that you are 'ready' yet to be a senior writer. After all, it takes more than time and the juiciest of assignments to accomplish that. It takes a certain talent, an ability to turn the ordinary story into an extraordinary one!" He seemed to savor the cutting words. Ever since his first day at *Rendezvous*, there had been animosity between him and Shane. She sensed it without understanding the whys of it. "Now, be a good little writer and do as you're told. A good writer, in case you don't know," he added archly, "is supposed to see the opportunity for excellence in an apparently routine assignment."

As she shook her head in exasperation, her shoulder-length chestnut hair brushed against the beige suit jacket she wore. "All right, I'll do your fluffy story. And when my copy is in print," she vowed, "no one will pay more than scant notice to the fact that the issue of the magazine under discussion has an interview with the President in it!" With that, she spun around and stalked out of the conference room.

That was a dumb vow, Shane, she told herself as she marched into her office. She slammed the door so hard that the glass threatened to shatter and fall at her feet. Banks had given her this assignment to hurt her pride. He knew how much she wanted that presidential interview. He had been dangling it in front of her like a carrot for the last two months. But she had picked up the gauntlet. And she felt herself more than equal to the challenge he had hurled her way. Damn Banks, though! She sighed.

Frustrated, she sank into her chair and ran her hand absently over her typewriter. They had come a long way, this typewriter and she, all the way from Hunter College, an eternity ago. She looked out the window at the cloud-strewn sky and imagined the hundreds of scurrying figures on the busy New York street twenty-two stories below. She'd come such a long way just to write a story about some so-called "hunk" who was probably as mindless as he was supposedly gorgeous? What a waste of her intellect, her journalistic ability! She hit the keys of the typewriter. Four keys tangled—captured in mid-flight to the platen.

She flicked the keys apart, and was staring at her grease-blackened fingers when the door opened. Meg, her short, slightly overweight blond secretary, looked at her a little uncertainly.

"Should I be waving a flag of truce?" she asked, peering around the room, then at last fixing her gaze on Shane's scowling face.

"I'm really just mad at myself," Shane confessed. "So come on in." She shrugged. "Honestly, Meg, I should have realized that Banks would never give me that assignment. He thinks only men are capable of interviewing presidents."

Meg's wide face broke out into a sunny smile. "Personally, I think you got the better end of the deal! Just think." She paused, gave a long sigh, and allowed the expression on her face to grow wistful, dreamy. "Oh dear Lord . . . to be with Nick Rutledge . . . even for a day. Why—"

"Wait a minute," Shane interrupted. "Rutledge is just a man like any other. He puts his pants on one leg at a time."

"Yes, but what legs . . ." Meg's voice trailed off.

"Meg, knock it off. He's a product of Hollywood hype, that's all. Sure, he's probably good raw material in the looks department, but don't forget he's got an excellent makeup man and an excellent lighting technician at his disposal. If you ran into him in the grocery store—if he were the checker, or the butcher—I bet you'd hardly notice him," Shane said. "How much you want to bet the guy's a runt and they either dig a hole for his leading ladies to step down into or provide a stepstool for him to climb up on?" She snorted. "Probably has a Napoleonic complex to complement his subnormal IQ and stud mentality."

"Oh, Shane," Meg wailed. "So cynical. So unkind. That's not like you."

Shane relented. "Sorry Meg," she said humbly, a warm gleam in her eyes for her fellow employee and friend. "I'm just licking my wounds . . . or opening them. It's time for the phoenix to rise out of the ashes. I'm going to make a damn good story out of this! Just wait until Banks sees the job I do!"

Meg slipped out of the office as Shane stared across the room at nothing in particular, but with a triumphant grin on her face.

It was raining when Shane landed in Denver.

"Anderson gets a secret service man to meet him, I get rain," she muttered. She juggled two suitcases that had taken her half an hour to retrieve from the luggage-hungry but lethargic maws of the baggage-handling system. Passengers jostled her on either side, all apparently in a hurry to cross over into the Denver city limits. But Shane refused to rush. This assignment was going to take a long time. Why should the prisoner race to her jail sentence?

People were scrambling for taxis, so she set down her suitcases and waited for a few minutes before whistling loudly to get a driver's attention. Soon she was sitting inside a dry cab, the musty smell of the cab driver's wet wool sweater encompassing her. And even sooner, it seemed, she was standing before the registration desk of the Plaza Cosmopolitan Hotel, where a rather frantic young man in a green-and-white sweater asked questions of the man behind the desk.

Shane drummed her fingers and let her gaze wander aimlessly around the lobby. Suddenly, though, she was caught up short.

"Don't you have a reservation for a Mr. Shane McCallister?" the youth at her elbow asked.

Shane turned to stare at him. He was an amiable-looking guy of about nineteen, with a thatch of blond hair that kept falling into his eyes as he spoke.

"The magazine said he'd be here. And I already missed him at the airport," the young man said, apparently trying to read the guest register even though it was upside down. "Could you check and—"

Shane put her hand on his shoulder. "I'm Shane McCallister."

The heads of both the desk clerk and the young man swiveled in her direction. After a moment's perusal the desk clerk displayed only mild interest; the young man, however, was riveted—and obviously quite surprised. "You—you're Shane McCallister?"

"Yes."

"But you're not a man!"

"Really?" she asked wryly. "Sorry to disappoint."

His eyes swept over her curvaceous body, came to rest on her face, then blinked rapidly in embarrassment. He awkwardly stuck out his hand, wiping the palm first on the denim covering his thigh. "Hi. I'm Scottie."

"Well, Scottie," Shane said patiently, shaking his hand, "what can I do for you?"

"It's what I'm supposed to be doing for you!" he said, with such an earnest and emphatic inflection that Shane could scarcely repress a smile. "I was supposed to pick you up at the airport, but I was looking for a man with a press card—"

"Tucked into a reporter's slouch hat?" she asked, amused. "Ah, Scottie, I can tell you've been watching too many 1940s movies on television."

He grinned. "Well, nobody described you, and—"

"Why don't you tell me the rest of it in the car?" she asked abruptly. She'd glanced at her watch, noting that it was almost four, and she'd hardly have time to get to the set and meet her quarry if they didn't hurry. She waved away his comment and hastily checked in, asking to have her bags taken to her room. Then she turned back to Scottie, a brilliant smile from her putting him at ease. "Lead, on, MacDuff," she said . . . and he did, straight through the lobby and out to a limousine drawn up to the curb. Well, Shane thought, at least she'd be riding in style.

"I'll sit up front with you," she announced, then let him open the passenger door for her.

Scottie slid into the driver's seat, his manner a little more relaxed. "Boy, is Nick going to be in for a surprise," he told her.

"Why?"

"He was expecting a guy," Scottie told her with a chuckle. "I never knew any girl, um, lady named Shane before."

She understood and smiled. "My father was planning on a boy. Once I made my appearance, the name just stuck."

She looked out the window as they reached Denver's outskirts and kept going. The windshield wipers worked overtime on the large raindrops, slapping them away just in time for the next set to take their place. "Where are you shooting?"

"Due south of Denver, just outside of Kiowa. We were at a standstill when I left," he told her, "what with the rain and all."

She nodded, taking out her pad. No time like the present.

"Tell me all about Nick Rutledge," she said in a confidence-inspiring, enthusiastic tone.

"He's just the best there is," Scottie answered, his face beaming as his voice, too, brimmed with a smile.

Shane studied his guileless profile for a moment. Of course he'd say something like that. The pencil in her hand, poised above the pad, quivered. Damn. Nothing new in that angle . . . hm-m, yet! She smiled. Digging, she reminded herself. That's what it would take to make this report sizzle. Yes, digging. And letting everyone talk until a true picture emerged of this so-called movie god. Tentatively she entitled her article: "The Truth About Nick Rutledge."

"What is it you do for him, Scottie?"

"I'm a gofer." Scottie grinned. "I run errands for him, take care of little details, you know."

Shane suppressed a grimace. "Yes, I know, but do you earn enough money being a gof—I mean, doing these errands to live on?"

Scottie shook his head. "Of course not. I don't do this all the time, just summers. I go to school the rest of the year. USC," he added proudly.

"Oh, I see. I suppose your folks pay for that."

Scottie laughed, flipping a switch to set the windshield wipers on a slower speed. The rain had stopped pelting the car and was now coming at a steadier, more rhythmic pace. "My mom couldn't afford the University of Southern California. If it weren't for Nick, I wouldn't be going at all."

"Nick?" she repeated blankly.

"Yeah," he responded enthusiastically. He seemed to respond enthusiastically to everything, Shane noted. "He's paying for all of it. Not only that, but he sends money home to my mom and my two younger sisters."

Shane pounced on this information. Had Rutledge had an affair with Scottie's mother and was now paying her off with conscience money? She made a note to get in touch with the woman. "Why is he being so charitable?" she asked bluntly then.

"Charitable?" Scottie guffawed. "My dad was a stuntman in one of his movies three years ago. Got killed in a freak accident. Nick felt responsible."

Ah, an angle! "And was he?" Shane prodded.

"No," Scottie said, sounding surprised that she would even ask such a question. "Wasn't anyone's fault. Dad was doubling for Nick in a dangerous stunt with a real high leap at the end of it. There was a big wind factor he hadn't counted on, we guess, and somehow he missed the center part of the air bag. Broke his neck and just about everything else." Scottie was silent for a moment. "Nick had wanted to do the stunt himself, but the insurance people went berserk at the mention of it. So did the producer. Anyway, Nick knew the stunt was too dangerous and kind of felt he should have convinced them to let him do it. Then, if he had, Dad wouldn't have been killed. Nick was the one who came and told us about it. He was damned choked up . . . really, well, kind."

With his money, Nick could well afford to be kind, Shane thought, but nevertheless she was moved by Scottie's loss. "I'm sorry about your father," she murmured.

He shrugged, obviously trying to push away his sorrowful feelings. "Everybody's got to die sometime. Dad died doing what he liked best. He loved the business. So do I," he told her, his bubbly tone returning. "I'm studying to be a director."

Shane forced a smile. For a moment she was silent, looking out the window again, straining to see the terrain that was partially hidden from her by a curtain of shimmering rain. "I think I've arrived in the middle of your flood season," she said glibly, to lighten the mood.

"Yeah, the rain is pretty bad, isn't it?" Scottie agreed. "Nick's not too thrilled about this weather. We were ahead of schedule until today."

For the next twenty minutes he droned on and on about his idol. Shane took a few more notes and chalked off the rest of it as hero worship. Then they arrived at the set. Scottie brought the car to a stop as close as possible to the entrance of the main tent. He had no way of knowing that it was also next to a puddle of mud. Neither did Shane . . . until she stepped into it getting out of the car. Her right shoe slid into the oozing mass, the mud sucking at her toes through the open, high-heeled sandal.

Stepping gingerly onto harder ground, muttering an oath under her breath, Shane took it as an omen.

"Can I be of any help?"

The deep voice rumbled at Shane, surrounding her on all four sides. She didn't even have to look up and into his tanned face to know that voice belonged to Nick Rutledge.

# *Two*

Shane stood, lopsided, with the strap of her formerly light brown shoe dangling from her fingertips. Mud oozed from the shoe and plopped to the ground. Her right leg was splattered with a not-so-fine layer of mud, and she didn't even dare look down at her foot. It felt awful. She definitely wasn't putting her best foot forward to meet America's latest heartthrob.

Actually, she didn't meet *him;* she met his *chest.* When she turned toward the owner of that deep, resonant voice, the first thing she encountered was wall-to-wall chest barely covered by a white shirt that was slashed to the waist. Muscles rippled in all directions beneath the tanned skin.

"Cinderella, I presume," said the resonant voice, taking the shoe from her fingers.

For one of the very first times in her life, as she looked up into his face, Shane was at a loss for words. The man was obviously laughing at her, and she should have been annoyed with him, as annoyed as she was with Banks for sending her here in the first place. But his physical presence was rather overwhelming, and for the moment she was reduced to speechlessness.

The man's face was flawless—absolutely, completely flawless. It was only inches away; it was without the benefit of makeup or cunning lighting . . . and it was perfect. He really did look the same off-screen as on! His high cheekbones gave his face a sensual look that blended magnificently with the neatly trimmed Van Dyke beard and moustache he sported. The latter gave him a bit of a devilish quality, as did the slightly unruly deep brown hair that was just a tad away from straight. Even his nose was perfect, something that always struck Shane as an oddity. Noses hardly ever seemed to fit, being too large, too small, with nostrils too flared or pinched, or with a bump in the absolutely worst place. His was fashioned just right for his face. If the man had a plastic surgeon, he was the world's best, Shane decided. The only thing that kept Nick Rutledge from having "Perfect" stamped on his forehead was the fact that he had gray eyes. A face like that should have had sky-blue eyes. This was probably God's way of showing the world that no one is perfection personified. But Nick Rutledge came darned close. Shane decided he had to have a brain as quick as cold oatmeal. Anything more would be totally unfair.

She suddenly realized that while she'd been studying him, Nick had been doing some minute inspecting of his own. She tossed her proud head, the motion pushing her abundant hair over her shoulder. She couldn't help wondering how well she scored in his opinion, even while she told herself that the mere idea of rating high with him was utter foolishness. Still, she was not one to underestimate any of her attributes, and she knew that what Nick was seeing was a woman whom some had called beautiful. Her fine-boned face had a lingering allure, a power that whispered of her loveliness long after she'd left a room.

Nick's gray eyes, temporarily finished with their examination, shifted to Scottie, who still stood awkwardly at Shane's side. "You picked an awful day to bring your girl friend to the set, Scottie." He gave Shane a wide smile. "Let me see if I can help you salvage the situation. Here, take this to the prop area and have them clean it up," Nick told Scottie, handing him the shoe.

Shane was totally unprepared for what happened next. As Scottie hurried away on his mission, Nick scooped her up in his arms and carried her into the center of the activity, beneath the tent. She stared at him, openmouthed, trying not to think how good his arms felt around her.

"Mabel, I need a towel," Nick called out, depositing Shane on a blue studio chair. Almost reluctantly, she released her balancing hold from about his neck.

A nondescript person suddenly emerged from the background to thrust a towel into Nick's hand. He took it without ever breaking eye contact with Shane.

"What is it you think you're doing?" Shane demanded, finally finding her voice. She stared as Nick began wiping the mud away from her leg, using long, slow strokes. His strong fingers gently gripped her calf, sending all sorts of strange sensations colliding into one another.

"Getting you cleaned up, of course," Nick said innocently, as if he were unaware of the effect he was having on her.

Shane tried not to squirm as he reached up higher, going beneath her knee. She snatched the towel away from him. "I can do this myself, thank you," she informed him, hoping that the hot flush she felt was not visible. She took a deep, deep breath as she rubbed the towel over her leg.

Nick, squatting before her, simply watched. Shane grew self-conscious.

"Do you have to stare like that?" she asked, annoyed at her discomfort.

"Best-looking leg I've seen in a long time," Nick told her. "Too bad it belongs to Scottie," he murmured under his breath.

"It doesn't belong to Scottie," she informed him, almost haughtily.

"Oh, good; then, there's hope," Nick said, a twinkle in his eyes.

She stopped rubbing. "It belongs to *me*," she announced. Was this some throwback who considered women to be chattel?

"Even better," Nick said, taking the towel out of her hands. For a moment, his eyes held her prisoner of a nameless magic. She could feel her heart thumping erratically in response.

"Here's the shoe, Miss McCallister," Scottie called out, returning to the scene. "I'm really sorry."

"McCallister?" Nick echoed, looking very surprised.

It pleased Shane to unnerve him slightly. After all, it was only fair. He had unnerved her a great deal in only a few short minutes.

"I'm Shane McCallister," she told him, rising. Her delivery was spoiled by the fact that she tottered a little. Nick's fingers, strong as steel, gripped her elbow to steady her.

"I thought you were supposed to be a man," he said.

"I failed the physical," she said dryly.

His eyes swept over the length and breadth of her, lingering for a moment on the appreciable swell of her breasts beneath the smoke-blue nylon blouse. "So I see." He looked amused at his own mistake, taking the shoe Scottie offered. "Here, let me," and, not waiting for an answer, he bent down and took her newly cleaned foot in his hand. In an effort to regain her equilibrium, Shane reached out and made a grab for Nick's head. Her fingers sank down into a soft mat of dark hair. Nick gave no indication of whether she was hurting him or not, and she subdued an urge to pull at the roots.

"You'll have to forgive my mistake," he said easily.

Dear Heaven! She'd never known that having someone touch the sole of her foot could feel so . . . so erotic. She worked at steadying her breath.

"All *Rendezvous* told me was that Shane McCallister was coming out to interview me, and with a name like Shane, I just naturally assumed you were a man."

"If I were a man, I wouldn't be here doing this interview," Shane said, trying hard to be dignified while nearly tottering over.

Nick had a powerful body. He rose slowly and the process was a little overwhelming. The ends of Shane's fingertips tingled as they threaded from his hair, along his neck and powerful back. She felt, too, as if he had touched her all over even though he hadn't touched her at all. "Well, Shane, you won't have to be doing it anyway. I've changed my mind. No interview," he told her, and stepped back out of the circle of her arms.

Was she supposed to *beg* him to do an interview she didn't want to do in the first place? She wasn't about to go back to Banks and say she'd washed out. "Wait, don't be hasty," she said, putting a hand on his arm in order to keep him from walking away.

Nick stopped. "Okay," he said, eyeing her closely. "Convince me." He folded his arms over his massive chest and made Shane feel as if she were standing before some eighteenth-century buccaneer. All around her, crew members were drawing in closer to watch.

"Why this sudden wavering from no to yes to no again?" she asked. There, let him be on the defensive for a minute.

But he wasn't. "Reporters lie," he answered simply. "In a weak moment, my agent talked me into giving an interview. But the truth is uninspiring to reporters, so they make up their own stories. Why should I help?"

Ball back in my court, Shane thought resolutely. "What about your fans?" she countered. "You haven't given a personal interview in two years."

"I'm very grateful to my fans," he said in a sincere way. Then one eyebrow rose into an arch like a cupid's bow. "What about them?"

"Don't you think that they deserve a story right from your own lips?" she asked. And what sensuous lips they were, her wicked mind added. What was getting into her? "I don't know if you are personally acquainted with our magazine, Mr. Rutledge, but we do in-depth profiles on people. It is an intimate, deep interview—"

"How intimate?" he asked slyly.

She chose to ignore his question and its obvious inference. "—and I never alter facts."

"Nice to know," he commented, then took a deep breath. "I like your perfume."

"Fine," she said dismissively. "Does that cinch the deal?" Who would ever believe that she was actually trying to talk a Hollywood personality into giving an interview? She had such high goals, such great aspirations. They included being in the eye of a hurricane, at the center of a volcano, on top of a world event—not mingling with tinsel-town people. But Meg had been right. Rutledge was a dynamic personality, and a story like this might be better even than an interview with the President. "Well?" she asked, trying to look appealing.

"We have a deal," he said in a sudden, inexplicable reversal. He reached for her hand and shook it. A wave of electricity shot through her body as his fingers curled about hers.

Shane smiled, relieved. "Good. Now, if you would be so kind as to direct me to your secretary or whoever has your schedule for the next month, I'll try to plan my life around yours—"

"I like that," he said, smiling in a devilish way.

That smile made her nervous, but she thought she hid it well. "Then, we have an understanding?"

"I hope so." The words were almost purred.

She was in deep trouble. She knew it by the way her insides felt. Everything was pulling into a tight, quivering knot. It was going to be a hell of a month. Better set him straight now, her mind warned, before it was too late. Too late for whom, she didn't bother exploring. "Mr. Rutledge," she said, lowering her voice as her eyes swept over the various people who stood well within earshot, "I am a professional, and I am here strictly for the purpose of doing an interview." There, that sounded firm. She congratulated herself.

But his eyes teased her, as if throwing her words back at her. "That remains to be seen. And my friends call me Nick." With that, he winked, and excused himself for a moment. Shane was left alone with a sea of curious eyes examining her. Then, slowly, the crew members began to amble away and resume their work.

"Didn't I tell you he was great?" Scottie asked.

Shane had forgotten about him. She seemed to have forgotten a lot of things in Nick's presence, like how to maintain her poise. She didn't like men who unnerved her. Until this larger-than-life character, the only other man who had accomplished that feat was Alan Sherman, and she had married him, much to her everlasting chagrin. Six months later, clutching her divorce papers in her hands, she had formed a hard opinion of overwhelmingly good looking men.

Shane let Scottie ramble on amiably as she tried to regain her outward calm, although nothing at the moment could cool the embers inside. Their heat came from the Rutledge mystique.

Nick returned in five minutes. "Gypsy's getting a schedule together for you right now," he said.

"Gypsy?" she asked.

"My secretary."

He would have a secretary named Gypsy, Shane thought. Somehow it fit.

"In the meantime, have you had dinner?" he asked.

"I had a sandwich on the plane," she told him.

"Sandwiches don't count," he assured her, taking her hand. She left it there for a moment, absorbing the warmth that seeped into her. Every movement of his was so . . . so personal, she thought. He acted almost as if they were old friends instead of virtual strangers.

"Wait a minute," she protested before she was whisked away. "Aren't you in the middle of shooting? How can you leave?"

"I can leave because we're not shooting. *The Lord High Protector* is supposed to be standing on the deck with the wind in his hair and the sun smiling down upon his sails," he explained humorously. "Nowhere in the script does it read that he's supposed to be drowning in the process. The weatherman says there's no relief in sight, so we stop shooting. Satisfied?" She nodded. "Good. Give me a minute to change—unless"—he paused, a smile curling the corners of his mouth—"you'd like to describe the way I get out of my costume—strictly for your article, of course."

She didn't like his laughing at her. Her face did not move a muscle as she replied icily, "The interview is not supposed to be that intimate."

The broad shoulders shrugged. "Too bad. Scottie, show Shane around the set and bring her back here to meet me in ten minutes."

"C'mon," Scottie urged. "You'll like everybody," he told her. Shane cast one disparaging glance in Nick's direction and followed Scottie. He introduced her to a host of cameramen, propmen, stunt men and women, and supporting actors. She tried hard to remember which face went with which name, because she fully intended to interview as many of them as she could in order to add weight and depth to a theory she was developing about Nick.

Shane had just met the wardrobe mistress when the sound of a female's loud voice pierced the air with a chalk-scraping screech.

"Liar!" the woman, dressed in a very revealing costume of the era, spat at Nick's retreating back. She kicked one of the light stands, sending it sprawling, then wheeled and stormed away.

"That," Nick said, taking hold of Shane's elbow, "is our temperamental leading lady, Adrienne Avery. She is your proverbial hellcat."

"What's she so angry about?" Shane asked. In the background she heard a series of crashes, diminishing in loudness. Adrienne was obviously kicking and destroying everything in her path.

Nick thanked Scottie, then hustled Shane across the set. He opened an umbrella and held it over her head as he guided her toward his car. "I promised Adrienne dinner," he mumbled.

"She must have been really hungry," Shane said wryly. "Look, I don't want to cause any problems," she protested. He was still holding her elbow, as well as the umbrella. In addition, somehow, he was managing to rub his forearm against her breast. His expression was innocent as a babe's, but Shane would have placed a bet that he knew exactly what he was doing. She was having trouble maintaining any semblance of coolness, inside or out.

He opened the car door. There was nothing to do but get in, which she did. "You don't have to take me out to dinner," she insisted.

"Oh, but I do," he said. Then he hastily went around the car and in on his side. "You've shown me the error of my ways," he told her, patting her leg. Actually, it was more like her thigh. Why did he have to keep touching her?

"I have?" she asked. Her throat felt dry.

"Yes, I should mingle more freely with the press," he said, starting up the Ferrari.

"I had no idea I was so persuasive," she muttered, trying to calm the dart of heat that was shooting through her from its point of origin on her thigh.

"Oh, but you are," the low voice assured her. "What's your pleasure?"

She wasn't sure she was hearing correctly. "What?"

"Food." Nick laughed as she squirmed uncomfortably.

If looks could kill, she thought, glaring at him, the man would be in the morgue in ten minutes. Eleven, tops.

"Do you like French, Chinese, seafood, what?" he asked.

"Seafood," she answered, grasping at the first thing that sounded right.

"Terrific," Nick acknowledged with a broad grin. "I know a fantastic restaurant with magnificent seafood and an even better atmosphere—it's dim, bordering on dark." His voice was almost seductive, she thought.

"Don't you like seeing your food?" she asked.

"Sure, but I like eating in peace better," he told

her. "In a well-lit, well-trafficked place, I spend more time signing autographs than I do chewing. And no matter how good it is, cold is not my favorite temperature for clam chowder."

That sounded fair enough, she thought, trying hard not to stare at him while he talked. But it was as if her eyes were hypnotically drawn to him throughout their ride. Etched in the fading light of dusk, Nick was almost unbearably handsome. She'd never thought she'd think that about any man, and certainly not in admiration. Handsome men used their faces to open doors for them, to deceive women. Whoa, hold it, no personal interjections here, she warned herself. Be professional. The man is innocent until proved guilty. She struggled to keep an open mind—and calm body.

The restaurant was charming, and the *maître d'* seemed genuinely delighted to see Nick. They were ushered to a very private corner table with a plush booth forming two sides of the dim nook. Rather than sit on the chair opposite her, as Shane had expected him to, Nick slipped into the booth alongside her. Her body stiffened slightly, alerted to the danger of having him so close, and when he asked her if she'd like a cocktail, she startled herself by ordering sherry. Good grief! What was the matter with her? She hated sherry. And of course it was served immediately, along with a glass of chilled chablis for Nick.

"You come here often?" she asked. Captivating question, she silently taunted herself.

Nick smiled, his smile penetrating her veins more swiftly than the sherry she'd just sipped. "Whenever I can. Don't forget, I live in Hollywood when I'm not on location."

She toyed with the stem of her goblet, avoiding the hypnotic effect of his eyes. It was bad enough that his cologne was assaulting her olfactory system—indeed, her nose was positively twitching. Never had a man's cologne aroused her so. The sherry must be going straight to her head, totally bypassing the airline's skimpy sandwich. "I understand you had complete control over casting and location. Why did you pick Colorado?"

The question seemed to please him. "There are certain locations here that look very romantic when the sun hits them just so. I think it adds a lot to the movie."

"Can't the sun 'hit just so' in California?"

"Maybe," he conceded, picking up a piece of bread and buttering it smoothly. Everything he did, he did smoothly, she thought, just the way he rolled his words off his tongue. "But I grew up in Colorado—"

"So you decided you'd throw the locals a little money?" she asked.

"Something like that," he said. Then he put down his knife. "Correct me if I'm wrong, Shane, but I'm getting definite vibrations from you."

Uh-oh, here comes the macho pitch, she thought.

"Why don't you like me?" he asked softly.

Her eyes grew wide. Was he as perceptive as all that? Was she as obvious as all that? What struck her most was that Nick appeared to sound sincere, as if it mattered to him that one, lone woman wasn't falling at his feet. Maybe it did matter, she thought. No conquest unturned . . . "I don't *dislike* you, Mr. Rutledge—"

"Nick," he corrected.

"Nick," she amended. "I'm just not quite sure how to take you."

"In whole doses," he said helpfully. His eyes danced over her features.

Shane lowered hers. "I think I'll have the shrimp salad," she said, lifting the menu between them. She could hear Nick's soft chuckle. It touched every nerve ending she had. She pushed the sherry farther away from her.

The waitress came and went, as did their dinner. Time slipped away, and Shane got nowhere with her interview. Every question she framed sounded stilted, amateurish. It was a bad evening for her. She'd sound better in the morning, she reassured herself. So she turned down his next offer.

"Would you like to go dancing?" he asked as he put a large bill on the table and helped Shane out of the booth.

"I'd like to go to my room," she told him.

"That can be arranged." He stood behind her, a good foot taller than she was, his hands resting gently on her shoulders. She could feel the heat of his fingers penetrating her jacket. Somehow she knew they didn't have the same thing in mind.

"I meant alone."

"I'd never let a stranger go back to her lonely hotel room alone. Besides," he said, dangling the keys before her, "I have the car keys. Your coach awaits, milady," he said grandly.

Shane took his arm and went out into the night. It had stopped raining. There were a few stars sprinkled in the dark sky and winking down on the Friday-night activity, which was just beginning.

"You're sure you want to go back to the hotel?"

Nick asked again as the Ferrari was brought around for them.

"I'm sure," she said firmly.

She wasn't feeling all that firm when he stepped out of the car with her at the hotel and followed her across the lobby and into the elevator. She had expected him merely to let her out at the front entrance, not to follow her upstairs. But here she was at her room and here he was, right behind her. The tingling sensation was back.

"Well, this is my door," she said, fishing for her key. Why did keys always sink to the bottom of purses?

"Very nice door," he commented impishly. "Is the other side as nice?"

"I imagine so. Probably the same color and everything," she replied, amused despite herself.

"Really?" He sounded as intrigued as if she had just told him a deep, state secret. "I'd like to see it."

She laughed as she opened it. "See?" She held it for his inspection.

"Yes, I do see," Nick said, looking only at her as he closed the door behind him.

Shane fumbled for the light, missing the switch on her first swipe at the wall. The lamp on a nearby coffee table flicked on, and she almost sighed audibly.

Nick's gray eyes watched her steadily as she moved quickly into the room. "I don't leap at moving targets, if that's what you're afraid of."

She lifted her chin defiantly. "I'm not afraid," she informed him coolly.

"Then, come here," he said, his voice as inviting as a touch of velvet.

Shane found herself moving toward him, as if she had no control over her own legs. "We're supposed to be maintaining a professional relationship here," she heard herself protest, but the words came out with a lot less force than she had intended.

"Lady, you talk too much," Nick said as he took her face in both hands. His lips touched hers, at first, very, very gently. So gently that she thought she was dreaming. But as the pressure increased with the passing of seconds, Shane knew that this was no dream. This was quite real. Suddenly, doors that had been firmly shut five years ago sprang open, letting loose emotions she had been careful to bury. Horrified, she caught herself and pushed him back.

"That is not the way to end a kiss, Shane. You kind of taper off. You don't use a body block," he said, highly amused. "We're going to have to practice that."

"We're not 'practicing' anything," she informed him, her voice shaky.

"Rehearsals can be fun," he assured her, drawing closer.

Shane stepped back. "This show just had its final performance."

"We'll sponsor a revival," he told her, his eyes sparkling down into hers.

She tried another approach. "Look, I'm very tired." She marched to the door and opened it. Her message was clear.

"You didn't kiss like a tired lady," he said, grinning. He ran a finger along her jaw, resting it on her chin. "I think I'm going to like having an in-depth interview done." His eyes caressed her once more. "Sweet dreams," he murmured, then left.

Shane locked the door, leaning against it. A deep sigh escaped her lips. The fire of his kiss still burned.

# *Three*

A brisk, staccato knock echoed its way into Shane's consciousness.

She bolted upright in bed. Was she dreaming?

The knock came again, louder.

She groped for the clock, nearly falling between the bed and the nightstand. Six-oh-seven. Six-oh-seven? There was someone up at six-oh-seven? In the morning? On a Saturday? She tried to clear away the cobwebs from her mind and become lucid as the knock grew stronger. Maybe the hotel was on fire! "Oh, Lord," she muttered, grabbing her violet negligee as she jumped out of bed. Her feet searched for her slippers and came up with only one. One was better than none, she thought as she hurriedly secured her filmy robe at her small waist. Quickly she unlocked the door and threw it open, expecting to see some flush-faced hotel employee ready to rush her out of a burning inferno.

Instead Shane found herself swept up into an embrace one moment before her mind registered just who was standing in her doorway. Her mouth was covered with forceful lips that seemed to suck her very breath away in a flash of pins and needles that danced up and down her arms and legs. For one wild moment she felt herself being carried away, savoring the deliciousness of the kiss. It tasted wonderful. Wait! What was happening here? In an effort at self-preservation, Shane wedged her hands up between herself and the assailant. With a mighty shove, she broke free.

Nick! Who else?

"What do you think you're doing?" she demanded. She realized that he wasn't looking at her face, and she glanced down. Her robe was now opened, and the gauzelike nightgown did very little to hide her contours and nothing to hide the fact that her nipples were almost standing erect with excitement. She wrapped the robe about herself quickly, securing the sash so tightly that it almost hurt.

"I just wanted to know if you kiss as well in the morning as you do at night. You do—but we're really going to have to work on your endings," Nick told her, strolling into the room.

Shane shut the door behind him. "You are the most egotistical, insufferable—" She broke off in annoyance with herself. An extensive vocabulary at her disposal, and all she could do was stutter like some blithering idiot!

Nick held up a finger. "Now, now, I didn't say *I* kissed well. I said *you* did. In case you hadn't noticed, that was a compliment."

Shane ran her fingers through her hair, pushing it out of her face. "I don't notice anything at six in the morning. Any decent person should be in bed at this hour!"

"I'm for that," Nick said. To her horror, he walked over to her bed and started to take off his denim jacket.

"That wasn't an invitation!" she said sharply, placing herself in front of him to stop his progress toward her bed.

Nick snapped his fingers. "Too bad." He peered over her shoulder at the rumpled bed. "You always sleep that messy?" he asked, nodding toward the sprawled covers. The pillowcase was half off, exposing a faded flower design.

Shane moved jerkily, suddenly self-conscious. He was starting in again, making her strangely unsure of herself. Oh, why hadn't she gotten a good night's sleep? Then at least she would have been fortified against him. But something told her that it would take a lot more than just a night's sleep to fortify her against *this* man. She plucked up the pillow and shoved it back in its case. "Can we keep my sleeping habits out of this, please?"

Nick went on as if she hadn't said anything. "Me, I sleep like a log for about five hours. That's all your body needs, really. The rest of the time is wasted, unless, of course"—he paused, his seductive eyes intent on her chest as she took in each breath; Shane felt as if her very cleavage was drawn to him—"unless you're not alone. Then it can be spent very fruitfully." He took her hand in his.

She wasn't up to fighting off the warmth his touch generated, so she unceremoniously pulled her hand free before the magic began to work.

"I'm not interested in bearing fruit," she said. From the grin on his face, she realized that her choice of words was poor, to say the least. "What are you doing here?" she demanded again.

"I've come to introduce you to the dawn, Shane. I have a strong suspicion you've never seen it."

"Dawn?" she echoed, her voice just a touch hysterical. "The sun coming up. Big deal."

"Oh, but it is," he assured her, ever so gently gliding his hands over her shoulders. He melted the fabric away.

Steady, Shane, steady. The man's a nut. She took a step back, away from his hands, away from her increasing vulnerability. "You're crazy, do you know that? I'm standing here, in my nightgown—"

"So I noticed," he cut in. She could almost hear the leer in his voice.

"—carrying on a wild conversation with a crazy man who never seems to sleep. Are all you Hollywood people like this?"

"I'm unique, remember?" He winked at her. "That's why you're doing this story. Remember?" He shoved his hands deep into the pockets of his well-cut, form-fitting jeans. Shane's eyes were inadvertently drawn to them and the way his muscular thighs were outlined against the well-worn material. In contrast, his hips were slim. Definitely the body of an athlete, she thought. The low-slung cut of the jeans led her mind in other directions. She reined in abruptly, jerking her head up. From the grin on his face, she knew he had been enjoying her appraisal. He pulled a paper out of his pocket and unfolded it before holding it out to her.

"What's this?" she asked, snatching the piece of white bond.

"You wanted my schedule for the next month, remember? Gypsy typed her little fingers to the bone, just for you."

"Probably her first experience with a typewriter," Shane said dryly. Why was she taking out her frustration on some poor woman she had never met? It was Nick who was making her so uncomfortable, not some woman with the improbable name of Gypsy.

Shane scanned the list. The first thing she saw was: Saturday, September 10th, Gloria's party. Bring Shane. That was today.

"What's this?" she asked him, jabbing her forefinger at the words.

Nick moved around to look over her shoulder. "Oh, that. You'll like it," he assured her, resting his hand comfortably on her shoulder. "Gloria gives terrific parties. She's one of my oldest backers."

Quickly Shane reviewed all the clothes she had brought along. "I'm not prepared for a party," she protested.

"Just bring yourself," he said. "That's being prepared enough." His hands started running over her shoulders again. She stiffened, trying to prevent his touch from affecting her.

"Hey, you're all tense. I can feel the knots standing out three inches high. Here, let me," he proffered, and without further comment, he went on to do just what she didn't want him to. He began to massage her, kneading her tight muscles and playing havoc with her insides.

She felt herself being lulled into almost a trancelike state as his hands reached higher and higher along her back, rubbing and stroking their way along the sensitive sides of her breasts. Shane sucked in her breath, fully intending to move. But she stood where she was, absorbing it all, craving it all.

Slowly, he turned her around, his hands barely brushing against the outline of her breasts, making every nerve in her body stand at attention. He tilted her head back with the point of one finger and his lips were on the smooth white plane of her throat, sending a throbbing ache all through her. She took shorter and shorter breaths as her robe fell off her shoulders, its absence not noticed as his mouth rained down soft kisses in its stead.

Nick's caresses were raking the embers of desire, long buried in the smoldering ashes of her past, and making them flame into a new and even brighter blaze. No, no, not again, a feeble voice inside her cried.

Bells. She was hearing bells. The telephone! She felt herself being released, albeit reluctantly. Was the reluctance his—or hers?

"Your phone," he said softly, nodding toward the intruding sound.

Shane clutched at it as if it were her lifeline back to sanity. "Hello?" Was that her voice? It sounded so shaky. She damned herself for its breathless quality and averted her eyes from Nick's knowing face.

"Oh, I'm sorry, Shane. I forgot about the time difference. Did I wake you?" It was Meg.

Thank God for Meg, Shane thought. "No, that's all right. I wasn't in bed."

"Almost," Nick whispered into her other ear.

His breath swirled about her neck and caused another emotional earthquake. Distance. She needed distance from this man. She grabbed up the white phone and went as far away from Nick as the long cord permitted—which was halfway into the tiny bathroom. The cord was long enough to hang out a good-sized line of wash on.

"I couldn't wait to find out. What's he really like?" Meg asked breathlessly.

"Like nothing you'd ever imagine," Shane said before she could stop herself. A chuckle from the other room drifted into the bathroom. "Look, I can't talk right now, Meg. Let me call you back, okay?"

"Fine, I'll be—" Meg never got a chance to finish her sentence as Shane hung up. She marched back into the other room, determined to get Nick out before something else happened.

His smile grew brilliantly inviting as he watched her put the telephone back on the nightstand. "Now, where were we before we were so rudely interrupted?" he asked, coming toward her.

"I was throwing you out of my room," she replied.

He picked up one thick curl that tumbled provocatively to her shoulder and kissed it lightly. "That's not quite how I remember it," he murmured. His smile softened as a thought seemed to hit him. "I bet you're as pure as the newly fallen snow."

"The condition of my 'snow' is none of your business," she retorted. What gave him the right to be so damned personal *all* the time? He was ruining her own image of herself as a professional. She wondered if Barbara Walters ever had to put up with something like this.

But Nick wasn't deterred by her cold voice. "Haven't you ever been involved with anything except your work?"

"I'm supposed to be asking all the questions, remember?" she said. But Nick said nothing, apparently waiting for her to answer him. After a beat, she shrugged. "I was married once," she said, trying to sound offhanded about it.

"And?" Nick asked, waiting. His voice was kind, drawing her out.

What did it matter? she thought as she turned her back toward him and looked at the rays of dawn filtering through her window. It had all happened a long time ago, to someone else, someone highly impressionable and vulnerable. "Alan was a handsome god with feet of clay and a girl behind every door. It lasted six months. I never understood why he bothered getting married. It obviously wasn't his forte."

She felt the heat of Nick's body as he stepped close behind her. For a moment, not a word was spoken as he softly stroked her hair. No, no pity. That was the worst thing of all. She squared her shoulders against his touch, then swung around.

"So much for true confessions. Now, since you've gotten me up, I might as well shower and get dressed."

"Fine by me," Nick agreed. "Need anyone to scrub your back?" The devilish rogue was back, flirting with her from beneath lavishly fringed gray eyes.

"No, and I'm not getting dressed with you sitting here. Go down to the lobby and wait for me," she instructed. She wondered how many women would dare to talk this way to him.

"The lobby?" he asked, feigning horror. "Madam, do you realize what awaits me down there?"

"What?" she asked, playing along.

"Why, there might be legions of my fans downstairs by now," he said, still using dialogue that might have sprung out of one of his costume dramas.

Shane sighed. "If you're swept away, I'll understand. I'll find you. Never fear."

"That's not the problem."

"Then what is?" she asked impatiently. *He* was the problem, she thought, and smiled grimly at him.

"Why, they might just surround me and tear off all my clothes. It's been known to happen, you know. You wouldn't want to go anywhere with me naked, would you?" The grin spread, covering every handsome inch of his face. "Or would you?" he asked, rakishly cocking his head.

Shane threw up her hands. She knew she was beaten before she even started. "All right, stay, then!" she snapped. She felt helpless when he poured on the charm; he'd done it from the first moment she met him, and she didn't like it one bit.

Angrily she snatched some clothes out of her suitcase, clothes she had meant to hang up last night but hadn't. Consequently, wrinkles that were supposed to have fallen out overnight now winked back at her as she eyed them. This was not going to be one of her better days, she just knew it. Hoping she had everything she needed, she barricaded herself in the bathroom, making sure she flipped the lock loudly.

"I'll behave," Nick's sensuous voice assured her through the closed door.

"When pigs can fly," she muttered, switching on the water in the shower. No hot showers for her today. She didn't need anything to lull her senses. She needed all her wits if she was to prevent herself from becoming another of Nick Rutledge's conquests. She was here for a good story that would result in the kind of attention that would advance her career. The last thing in the world she needed or wanted was to get emotionally involved with a Hollywood heartthrob who was half man, half god.

And very, very desirable, a tiny voice added as cold water pelted her body.

By the time she emerged from the shower, she felt a bit like an icicle, but at least her mind was functioning again. She made a mental outline of the questions she wanted to ask him and the points she wanted to look for. With sure fingers, she applied the light makeup she usually wore. Never overadvertise, she had learned. Subtlety got her point across much better.

But subtlety was going to have to fall by the wayside as she realized that she had neglected to bring her bra from the other room, and now the blue-gray jersey adhered tantalizingly to the full, firm outline of her breasts, leaving only the tiniest bit to the imagination of the beholder. Damn that man, she couldn't even dress in peace. Shane sighed. A lot of women went braless, she told herself, hesitantly opening the door. A lot of women also went sky-diving, but that didn't mean she had to be one of them. In addition, going braless before Nick was a little like waving a goldfish before a piranha. The alternative was to get her bra. Bad idea. The goldfish was just going to have to put on boxing gloves, she told herself firmly.

Maybe he wouldn't notice.

He noticed. One glance at his face told her it was the first thing that registered with him. He looked more than a trifle pleased. Shane feigned nonchalance as she sailed past him to her closet. The only things she had managed to put away last night were her shoes.

"Now what?" she asked in her best professional voice.

"Well, since we missed sunrise, what if we go to some nice, cozy nook for breakfast and you start to work. Wasn't that the agreement? You spend time with me and find out what typical days in my life are like?"

"Yes, that's the agreement," she said, wondering if all his days began with attempted seductions.

"Well, then, let's go," he said, handing her purse to her. "I've got a nice day in mind, and I'll have you back in plenty of time to get ready for the party."

He was leading again, she thought, but she had no choice expect to follow, which she did.

There were very few people in the lobby.

"Where are all your worshiping fans who were supposed to tear off your clothes?" she asked wryly as he ushered her toward the revolving door. Several heads turned in their direction, an obvious question shining in their eyes: Was that—?

"I guess they're still in bed," Nick said with a shrug. "Why? Were you looking forward to the sight?"

"Possibly," she conceded, then added with a touch of smugness, "It might have been nice seeing you defenseless against a group of women for a change."

"Women, Shane," he told her as a valet brought his car around, "are never defenseless, believe me. Each one of them has the ability to hold a man in the palm of her hand."

That wasn't the way she had heard it, she thought, thoroughly convinced that he was just trying to get her guard down. It made her twice as cautious.

The restaurant was charming, rather like a large, rambling country kitchen full of tables and chairs. There were only two or three patrons, and the waitress looked a little sleepy-eyed as she took their orders.

Shane pulled her tape recorder from her over-sized shoulder bag, pressed the "play-record" button and turned her attention to her assignment.

"It's been said that you've brought romance and light fantasy back to the silver screen. How do you feel about that?" she asked.

"It's not me, Shane," he said forthrightly. "It's the type of stories I choose to do. People need to believe in heroes and derring-do again. There's so much grim realism to deal with everyday, and, just like in the thirties, people need to escape from it occasionally. They need to go to another time and place for two hours, to become enveloped in something nobler, finer, more meaningful than weeds, mortgage payments, and price escalations. Sometimes they break off a piece of the feeling they get and carry it with them after the movie's over. That's all I want my movies to accomplish."

"To fill them with empty dreams?"

"Dreams don't have to be empty," he insisted. "But first they have to *be*. You have to have a dream in order to fulfill it," he explained when she looked at him quizzically. "I show them that hope and optimism still exist, that things *can* be overcome if they only try."

"Isn't that rather cruel?" Shane prodded, furrowing her brow. "What if they lose?"

"How will they know unless they try?" he countered. "You've got to risk a little to gain a little—sometimes to gain a lot."

"And sometimes you lose a lot," she pointed out.

He conceded that. "Yes, you do, but sometimes that extra ounce of optimism helps get you over the brink. There're two ways to look at anything." He raised his glass of water. "Describe this to me."

"It's a glass of water," she answered dismissively.

"And?"

"It's clear," she added, knowing exactly what he was driving at.

"And?" he persisted.

"All right! It's half empty."

"Aha. I see it as half full," he told her, putting the glass down.

Shane shrugged. "Either way, there's only half the amount that there should be."

"Yes," he pointed out, "but you lament the half that's gone. I rejoice at the half that's left."

"You must be very easy to shop for around Christmas," she said drolly. "Just how did someone with your noble thoughts get into this line of work?" She was acquainted with the usual Hollywood stories but wanted to hear it retold in his own words. She realized that despite her attempts to cling to her professionalism, she truly liked the sound of his deep, resonant voice. For a moment, she could see him on the stage, hear his eloquent voice delivering a soliloquy from a Shakespeare play.

"I got into it by accident," he confessed. The waiter brought their orders, and Nick cut into his sausage with gusto. She waited several seconds before he continued. "I was going to USC, and a friend of mine was eager to read for a new director. Johnny was always on the alert for cattle calls— that's when they call down a large group of people and weed out the ones they don't want," he clarified for her benefit. "It was a two-man part, and Johnny thought he'd do better if he had someone to read with him, so I went along. I really think he was a lot better than I was," he said, and dug into his food again. She waited for him to finish the second sausage. "Anyway," he went on, wiping his mouth—she fought the urge to do the job for him—"Johnny got the part he was after, a twelve-liner. The director took me to John Bowman, who was casting the lead in *Robin Hood*. Something clicked and I was on my way." He made it sound so simple.

"What were you doing at USC?" she asked, toying with her own food. Somehow, when she was around Nick, she kept forgetting to eat.

"Studying to be a lawyer," he confessed. She looked surprised, and he laughed. "Lawyers need good memories too, so memorizing lines comes easy to me. Besides, being an actor is a lot more fun. I like swinging from mastheads and playing

Errol Flynn," he confided with a wicked wink, one that would have done Errol proud, she thought.

"Then it's a game to you?"

"Rather a serious game," he said, "when the paychecks of X number of people depend on your doing a good job and doing it on time. No, I take my work very seriously. I just enjoy it. That's what life is all about"—he paused and there was only a hint of a twinkle in his eyes now—"finding what you like to do and doing it."

"You're lucky you can follow your philosophy."

He took her hand, pressing it gently. "Yes, I am."

Shane's uneasiness returned.

# *Four*

He brought her to his home.

When he first suggested it, Shane had antici-
pated a small, secluded apartment. She was not
prepared for the large, contemporary, wood-and-
glass two-story house standing on the crest of a
mountain above Denver.

"I thought you said you lived in California," she
said as she looked around the massive living room,
with its plush, light blue carpeting. She felt her
heels sinking in. The pile was almost engulfing
her three-inch heels, the same way Nick's personality was engulfing her, she thought.

"I do, but this is home. I'm a native Coloradoan,
remember?" The pressure of his hand on her
shoulder blades urged her forward.

"Yes," she muttered. That was on the first tape
somewhere. She looked up at the huge vaulted
ceiling, wondering what a person could do with

all this living space. Her tiny apartment could fit in this one living room, with enough room to spare for a volleyball court.

Nick came around in front of her, striking a grand pose as he leaned against the oak banister of his long, winding stairway. "Welcome to my humble abode," he teased.

"Just what is your definition of humble?" she asked, still drinking in the decor. Rather than being overpowered by it, she found it surprisingly tasteful and subdued, the colors a pleasing blend of blues and browns. She had never thought the two colors could complement each other so well.

"Humble is what I feel when I'm next to you," he said, swinging down from the bottom step and neatly taking hold of her waist. She half expected a long vine to pop out of the ceiling so he could sail with her in his arms.

"I think you've been studying your lines in those movies too closely," she commented, trying to let him know that she was not affected by his charm.

"Hi."

Shane turned around and saw Scottie coming toward them. He was wearing a robe and brown-dotted pajama legs poked out below its hem.

"I didn't know you were an early riser like Nick," he said, joining them.

"Not voluntarily," Shane said. "Do you live here?" There was no other conclusion to be drawn at the moment, but she would have thought it more fitting if a bevy of scantily clad girls was to come spilling out of secluded bedrooms. One sleepy-eyed young man didn't do much to enhance an exposé.

"I promised his mother I'd look out for him," Nick told her, answering for Scottie.

She looked up at Nick's face, which never seemed to be far away from her own. "You're sounding nobler all the time," she said dryly.

"But of course. Was there ever any doubt?" Nick sounded as if he might be serious.

Shane did not answer his half-posed question. Instead she began to meander the length of the brightly lit foyer, looking at the paintings that hung there. An enormous skylight loomed above on the second floor.

"Can I show you around?" Nick offered. Once again he slipped an almost possessive hand around her small waist, pulling her closer to him, so her breasts rubbed against his rib cage. "Perhaps you'd like to see my casting couch? All of us nasty Hollywood types have one, you know. It's where we seduce innocent young things." He raised and lowered his brows twice, twirling the edge of his moustache villainously.

Scottie laughed, then excused himself to get breakfast.

"I think we'll skip the couch," Shane said, backing out of his embrace. "I'm sure you don't use anything so archaic." She cocked her head, thinking for a moment. "You'd be the type to improvise."

Nick's eyes sparkled as he led her away. "The stars above, the new-mown hay—anything at my disposal," he told her, whispering the words into her hair.

A little shiver went through her. She could scarcely pay attention during the tour of the house, but she did learn that there were twenty rooms in all. From the decking outside the second-story game room, Shane looked down on a valley dotted with houses and cars. She let out an impressed soft whistle.

Nick grinned. "It is kind of like looking down from a castle, isn't it?" he asked, reacting to her expression.

She turned toward him, finding him even more magnificent than the view below her. She leaned against the intricately fashioned railing, with its fleur-de-lis motif. "Maybe you're taking your roles to heart," she suggested. He was moving in to kiss her. She could read the thought in his eyes. She turned her head and looked back down at the valley. "Aren't you afraid of getting type-cast?" she asked, a bit too quickly.

He laughed. Was it at her action or her words? "I already am," he told her. "And it doesn't bother me one bit. I have no great ambition as an actor. I know what I'm capable of, and when the time comes when I can no longer scale mountains to free young damsels in distress, I'll move on to other parts. Right now, I'm having a ball. It's nice being paid for being a hero."

"Nice work if you can get it," Shane conceded, smiling. "Okay, now what?"

"Now I take you to my chamber of horrors," he told her glibly.

"Would you care to be a little more specific?" she prodded as he took her hand and led her from the terrace.

"I have a gym on the first floor," he clarified. "I try to work out at least a little each day. Pectoral muscles tend to disappear if you give in to a life of ease," he said, flexing his chest to emphasize his point. It looked rock-hard to her. "The studio heads would be very disappointed with a flabby hero," he added with a grin. "C'mon, you can watch."

If someone had asked Shane a week ago to name

five activities that would have bored her to tears, she would have put watching someone work out at the top of the list. Yet here she was, actually looking forward to seeing Nick go through his paces. She wasn't sure just what to expect. In a vague way she pictured some grunting and groaning, lots of sweating and clanging metal, yet there was still something about seeing that well-constructed body being honed to even further perfection that excited her.

Nick went to change, and she was alone in the large room, alone with mysterious tangles of machinery that were guaranteed to insure a good, professional workout. They all looked like instruments of torture to her. She ran her hand across one of the machines—how cold it was to the touch. The room was well lit, and three walls were mirrored floor to ceiling.

"Must like to see himself get sweaty," Shane said under her breath as she walked over the padded floor. An amused smile flitted over her face at the thought of the mirrors serving to highlight another activity. The floors was certainly comfortable enough for it.

What was wrong with her? Ever since she had set eyes on Nick, her mind kept drifting to intimate subjects. The next thing she knew, she'd be indulging in wild fantasies involving the man. She had always prided herself on being different. Mooning over Nick Rutledge, she told herself sternly, was definitely not different.

Shane was leaning forward against the ballet barre along the wall and trying to recall stretching exercises that had been part of her life when she was a teenager, when Nick entered the room. She caught his reflection first. Involuntarily, she sucked in her breath. He was wearing a net T-shirt with blue piping running along the armholes, and matching blue shorts. Some sort of sports shoes were on his feet, but who was looking at his feet? The rest of him was too magnificent for her to think of paying much attention to anything below his ankles. Shane couldn't understand why he thought he needed to exercise. Why tamper with perfection?

Slowly she turned around, trying not to be obvious as she appreciatively drank in his form. She *was* staring, looking for a flaw, a scar, *something* that would render this superb man more human. She failed.

"Have you ever thought of doing a remake of Tarzan?" she asked in an awed voice before her conscious mind could stop her.

The grin on his face took him down from Mount Olympus and into the realm of a devilish rogue, more human, true, but far more dangerous. "Tarzan's lines aren't romantic—but his moves are," Nick responded, his eyes petting her from across the room. "How would you like to play Jane?"

"I'm not good at climbing trees."

"Trees wouldn't be what you'd be climbing."

A hot blush blazed in her cheeks. "Um, what's this thing?" she asked quickly, turning away from him and pointing out a large piece of machinery.

Obligingly, Nick looked over to where she was pointing. "That's used to do arm curls without injuring the elbows. Mustn't damage the merchandise," he told her coyly.

"Is that how you see yourself?" she asked. "As merchandise?" How awful!

"No, I have too much self-respect for that."

He sat down on the padded seat and demonstrated the strange contraption. Shane watched, mesmerized, as the awkward position he assumed forced his abdominal muscles to tighten. "But," Nick added, "I'm too much of a realist not to know that that's partially the way the studio sees me. I work with the assets I have," he concluded matter-of-factly. He lowered the bar, his breath easy and steady. Just a little perspiration glistened on his shoulders. "You can sit over there." He pointed out a chair in the corner. "I promise not to take too long. This is all probably very boring to you."

She nodded and went to the chair, but mentally she disagreed with him. Nothing about him seemed to be boring to her. Finding a sharp, new angle with which to write her article was getting to be harder and harder. She definitely didn't want it to sound like a gushy movie magazine article, endlessly extolling his virtues. There had to be a chink in the armor, she told herself. But somehow, she wasn't all that anxious to find it any more. Less woman and more journalist, she reminded herself firmly. Taking out her pad, she sat with her pencil poised and ready, waiting for inspiration to strike.

The only inspiration that struck had nothing to do with writing a good story.

"How about a dip in the pool?" Nick asked, towering over Shane as he wiped the gleam of perspiration from his face. After his workout, his muscles bulged even more. Shane could see the definition of his stomach muscles through the net T-shirt.

She hastily closed her pad, which had gained nothing but three elaborate doodles in the last hour. "It's kind of cool outside for that," she said, trying to recall seeing a pool on the grounds. Its absence had struck her as a trifle odd at the time. She had thought a house this size would have one.

"It isn't outside," he informed her. "I've got an indoor pool right on the other side of the gym."

Shane rolled her eyes heavenward. "Doesn't everyone?" She followed him through the gym, trying to replace her pad and unused tape recorder in her bag. The objects fell with a thunk to the bottom of the shapeless brown purse as she hefted it over her shoulder.

The rectangular pool, with its crystal-blue water, shimmered invitingly, highlighted by another skylight. But there was a problem. "I don't have a bathing suit," she pointed out. Swimming and sunbathing had not crossed her mind when she had been packing for her trip.

"So?" he asked innocently. "I promise I won't look."

She didn't know whether to be annoyed or amused. What she did know was that she felt an electric thrill radiating through her.

"Even if you did look, there wouldn't be much to see," she said drolly. "I'm sitting this one out, thank you." She was about to drop her purse into a blue-and-white-striped lounge chair as she heard Nick say, "Can't blame a guy for trying." When she turned back to look at him, she saw him rummaging through a closet built into the side wall.

"Here," he said, producing something out of its innards that looked like tangled black string.

"Here what?" Shane asked, taking it from him.

"Here's your bathing suit," he told her.

She tried to smooth out the offering and stretch it across the important areas. There was hardly anything there. "This isn't a bathing suit," she protested. "It's a doily. Where did you get it?" Who was the last woman who'd worn it? Did he specialize in women who were size six?

"That's an undelivered gift," he told her. "The lady it was meant for went her separate way a long time ago," he said and Shane wondered if it was true. Who in her right mind would leave him? "Try it on," he urged.

There were all sorts of reasons why she shouldn't put it on, she told herself, standing in the adjoining powder room and tying the silken black straps behind her neck. So why was she doing this? She couldn't even swim. Where was her reason? Put your clothes back on, her common sense instructed her as she turned the doorknob and went out.

For one moment, the voice of her common sense retreated to less than a whisper as she basked in Nick's obvious admiration.

"See, I told you it'd fit. I have a good eye."

Which must be growing into an eagle eye, if it thrived on skin. Such self-conscious thoughts faded, though, as she took a good look at Nick. He was wearing even less than he had in the gym. Now he wore a bathing suit that added new meaning to the word "brief." It was a striking shade of blue and was tantalizingly molded to his body. Shane's pulse was doing strange things all on its own as Nick's extreme maleness telegraphed itself to her.

"Come here," he urged, stretching out one hand languidly. "Sit by me."

"I have a better view here," she told him. She cleared her throat. "I need to take in the atmosphere of this room." I need to stay away from you, she silently amended. Her senses were beginning to feel slightly drugged. Must be the humidity from the pool, she tried to tell herself. Shane McCallister didn't react to men this way, even if they were gorgeous. Especially if they were gorgeous. "It looks a little like a grotto," she told him, gesturing at the white statues of ancient goddesses that stood in niches in the far wall.

"All it needs is a water sprite," he said, rising to his feet in a fluid motion.

Nick took hold of her hand and was drawing her toward the water. She had an inkling of what his intention was, before panic seized her.

"No, really, I don't think this is a good idea," she protested, "I—"

Playfully, he picked her up and threw her into the water, then dove in after her. She opened her mouth to protest more as she hit the surface. Chlorinated water rushed into her mouth, filling it and choking her. Her eyes stung, and she sank into the water, arms flaying. Her head pounded horribly, demanding air for her lungs, but there wasn't any. She was sinking, sinking. . . .

And then there was air, air all around her, cold and good. Gentle hands were placing her on something flat and hard. She was out of the pool. Her chest heaved, drawing in the sweet air, and she began to cough violently. When she finally opened her eyes, she saw Nick's concerned face looming over her. She was lying next to the pool, and he was brushing away the hair that was plastered against her face.

"Are you all right?"

She tried to nod. "Yes," she said in a raspy whisper.

"Why didn't you tell me you couldn't swim?" he demanded. "Lord, I'm sorry. Sometimes I do things impulsively."

She felt foolish as she shrugged her shoulders weakly. "I didn't want to admit it," she muttered. Then she noticed the three long red scratches on his arm. "Oh, no, did I do that?" she asked, sitting up shakily and touching the marks with hesitant fingertips.

"They'll heal," he told her dismissively. "Besides, I deserve them, and worse. I can't tell you how sorry I am."

His expression—one of concern mingled with apology—took all her self-righteous anger away. How could she berate him, when he was obviously feeling so badly about it? "I thought you were supposed to be perfect," she accused.

"Impulsiveness is my Achilles' heel. I usually know what I want right away and act on it." Nick stroked her cheek gently, his fingers gliding down to her chin. Pure desire blossomed in Shane's body. She was afraid that he could read the emotion in her eyes, and tried to look away, but Nick lifted her chin so that her eyes were level with his. Ever so slowly, his mouth descended to hers, making her taste his kiss before it had been born. The breathlessness that overtook her was totally different from what she had just experienced. This time her breath was a casualty to the delicious sensations that were overtaking her as Nick's kiss grew in magnitude.

He was on his knees, drawing her up against him, molding her soft contours against his hardening body, making her feel as if they were two halves of a whole. His hands were everywhere, stroking her wet skin and making it blaze with passion. She was aware of the fact that his lips had left hers and were now putting their mark on her flesh. Kisses rained lightly on her eyes, her cheeks, her throat. His tongue played momentarily with the beating pulse in the hollow of her throat, erotically arousing her even further. She felt her breasts tighten, the nipples forming rounded buds yearning to be caressed. Yearning for his touch.

As if reading her thoughts, Nick's next movement brought him down to the planes of her breasts. His large hands easily slipped the wet black material away from her alabaster skin, and he cupped each breast in his hands, sensuously rubbing them both until she was sure she was going to cry out. A restless movement flowed through her hips as she felt his tongue tease first one rosy nipple and then another.

His touch, though still gentle, grew more urgent as, once again, he pulled her against him. His lips pressed hard on hers, passion flowing from his mouth as their breaths mingled and became one. She was being absorbed by him, her own will disappearing into the swirling haze he created for her.

"Hi! You hungry—oh!"

Scottie's exuberant voice slashed the air. Reality crashed around Shane and she struggled for composure. Nick had released her and was now standing with his back to her, providing protec-

tive cover for her. Hurriedly she slipped the wayward bikini back in place and wished the flames in
her cheeks would die down.

"I—I brought sandwiches," Scottie said lamely.
As Shane turned around, rising awkwardly to her
feet, her knees still a bit weak, she noted that
Scottie didn't know what to do with his eyes. In
his hands, slightly tilted, was a tray full of different sandwiches. The cans of soda looked as if
they'd tumble to the ground any second. He
looked far more uncomfortable than she did, and
she rose to the occasion, stepping forward

"That was very nice of you," she said, taking
the other end of the tray. "I—I nearly drowned,"
she said, trying to sound matter-of-fact about it.
Yes, she had nearly drowned! Twice. "Your boss
thought it might be funny if he threw me in the
pool," she went on, setting the tray on the white
table between two of the chaise lounges. "Unfor-
tunately, I don't swim, and he had to rescue me."

"Mouth-to-mouth resuscitation can be reward-
ing," Nick told Scottie, who seemed to accept the
excuse without batting an eye.

As the three of them sat down to share the
sandwiches, Shane couldn't help wondering how
many scenes like this Scottie had walked in on
before. Something more than professional curiosity was being aroused here, she realized.

After a sufficient amount of time had lapsed,
Nick informed Shane that he was going to teach
her how to swim. Despite all her protests to the
contrary, Shane found herself back in the water.

"There's nothing to be afraid of," Nick assured
her. "Scottie is here for added protection."

She wondered if the twinkle in his eye gave his

words another meaning. What she needed protection from most of all was not the water, but herself. Nick had opened a Pandora's Box of emotion within her. She was shaken to the core and not at all sure she could handle those emotions. She tried to push those thoughts away and concentrated hard on the swimming pointers Nick gave. By the end of the session, she had managed to master floating.

A phone call interrupted the relaxed gaiety. Nick's opinion was needed on some last-minute script changes. "You want to come along?" he asked her after relaying the message to Shane. "You can record a little more of my life," he added with a wink.

She caught a reflection of herself at the bottom of the gleaming silver tray that Scottie had brought in earlier. Her hair, just beginning to dry, was a mass of tangled frizz. "No," she said, shaking her head. "If I'm to go to that party with you, I'd better see if someone can do something about this mess," she said, holding out one crinkled strand.

"Suit yourself," Nick said. "Personally, I think it's cute." With that, he kissed the top of her head and instructed Scottie to see about getting her home.

Shane watched him leave the room. There was a strange tightness in her chest that she tried to ignore.

# *Five*

Shane's hair swirled around her head, flagrantly defying her hairbrush in her efforts to get it to rest in its proper place. After her shopping trip, she hadn't found a beauty salon that would take her at such a late hour; she had to rely on her own resources. The gypsylike creature who stared back at her from the mirror told Shane that her resources weren't doing too well. She liked to wear her hair straight, parted in the middle. It gave her a cool, madonnalike quality. This hairdo made her look wild and reckless, as if she should be dancing barefoot and shaking a tambourine by a campfire.

"Fitting, isn't it?" she asked herself, surrendering the hairbrush to the shelf, and gave in to the inevitable. First he changed her cool interior and then he dumped her in the pool and went to work on her exterior. Two days around Nick Rutledge, and she hardly looked like the same person—or felt like her!

"And where is this all going to lead, pray tell?" she baited the self reflected in the mirror as she took the new cocktail dress from its box. "One month from now, all you'll be is a name to Nick Rutledge. Do you really want to get involved, maybe even fall in love, and then have it end in a month?" The reflection had no answers for her, just a very strange light in its eyes.

Shane sighed and wiggled into her dress. The front came down to a provocative V, while all that covered her bare back were two thin straps that crisscrossed, weaving their way down to her trim waist. The dress flared slightly from that point, with just enough material about her hips and legs to swish invitingly. She had bought it for the party. More than that, she had bought it to wear for Nick.

"Shane, there's nothing wrong with looking good," she told her reflection sternly. "But get off this merry-go-round before you fall off your horse reaching for that brass ring. Falling for a movie star doesn't have one sensible thing going for it. Now, write that article and keep your damned heart out of it!"

She was a doer, and hated waiting around, yet was always ready early. She sat down with her notebook in hand to formulate bits and pieces that would eventually go into the article. She had been resolved to write the best article possible. Now she couldn't write anything at all. An entire day wasted. This had to stop. She had to get hold of herself. She had always been able to control her emotions before, except for that brief period with Alan. And even then, she had been the one who filed for the divorce. She couldn't afford to fall in love again. The emotion ruined all the well-placed order in her life and definitely interfered with her goals.

A knock on the door interrupted the pep talk she was giving herself, the words fleeing as that now-familiar tingling took hold of her. Maybe, she thought, striding toward the door, she had been working herself too hard these last few years. She hadn't had a vacation. Maybe this wasn't a crazy kind of love she was heading for. Maybe it was just a nervous breakdown. Maybe—

Disappointment registered on her face as she swung open the door and found Scottie standing there instead of Nick.

"Boy, you look terrific!" he told her, his eyes bright.

Shane smiled, pleased. Maybe the wayward gypsy look was in. "Thank you. Couldn't Nick make it?" she asked, glancing up and down the hallway.

"Oh, he's in the car. He thought it'd be better if he didn't come out and cause a commotion," Scottie explained, "since he's dressed up."

"How's that again?" Shane asked, picking up a small cloth purse she had bought to go with her dress.

"People expect to see celebrities all dressed up, and that makes him easier to spot. If he's wearing faded jeans, people stand around and wonder, 'Is it or isn't it?' If he's dressed in a tux, they seem to know for sure."

"I guess that makes sense," Shane responded. She hadn't thought about how much privacy a celebrity gives up in exchange for that line of work. It was beginning to sound less glamorous all the time. She pulled the door shut behind her as Scottie led the way back to the elevator.

Nick waited for her in the back of the black limousine, the dark-tinted windows protecting him from the outside world. Shane felt as if she were entering an inner sanctum. Scottie closed the door behind her and went up to the driver's seat.

"Hi," Nick said warmly. Even in the dim light she could see the look of absolute appreciation in his eyes. "Very nice," he said huskily, moving closer to her.

"I found this dress in a little shop down the—"

"I was talking about you," Nick interrupted, touching her hair. "I like it like this. It gives you a wild, free look."

"As in fair game?" she queried uncertainly.

"I never indulge in games off the set," he told her, and Shane thought that he sounded sincere. But then, after all, the man was an accomplished actor. He could sound sincere selling her the Brooklyn Bridge or property in Atlantis.

"I see that this morning's near-drowning appears not to have had a permanent effect on you," he said. His gaze carefully washed over every inch of her.

Lord, he made her nervous. "None," she confirmed. "What's the occasion for the party?" she asked, feeling it wise to change the topic.

"It's Saturday," he told her.

"That's an occasion?"

"It is to Gloria," he said with a laugh. "She likes to have parties. Other people like to go to parties. It all works out," he told her easily. "You look very tense," he added after a pause. "Want another massage?"

The last thing in the world she wanted was for him to put his hands on her again. "No!" she said quickly, then added, "thank you," in a more subdued tone. "Besides, I should be working," she said, trying to sound a little more like her old self.

"You are working," he assured her. "You're getting to know me better." He slipped an arm about her shoulders.

"I mean really—"

"Well, if you'd like to get to know me in the biblical sense, that can be arranged too. We don't have to go to this party. . . ." His voice trailed off as his hand began to make lazy patterns on her bare back.

Shane pursed her lips. "I meant I should be asking you more questions."

"Ah, yes, more questions." Nick sighed. "All right, fire away."

"Are you interested in anyone very special at the moment?" she heard herself asking. Very professional, McCallister. The man's not dumb. He can see right through that one. A four-year-old could see through that one.

But Nick had the good grace to keep a straight face. "Yes, very special." His warm breath caressed her face, leaving no doubts in her mind as to his meaning. She liked his answer, yet couldn't quite bring herself to believe it. Not when Nick Rutledge could have his pick of any woman in the country.

"Shane, you're going to have to learn how to relax around me," Nick told her.

"Like this morning?" she asked archly.

His smile was beautiful. Men weren't supposed to have beautiful smiles. Men were supposed to be rugged, macho—yet Nick had a beautiful smile, she thought again. "This morning at the pool was nice," he said.

"This morning at the pool was a mistake," Shane said. She was uncomfortable and wanted to look him square in the eye yet didn't dare to. His eyes did those strange things to her.

"Okay," Nick said evenly. His tone surprised her. "Let's talk about it."

"I'd rather not."

He took her hand. "Kind of close-mouthed when it comes to your emotions, aren't you?"

She wanted to take back her hand, yet found that she had no power to do so. "I'm a careful planner," she said slowly. "I don't like becoming involved in things that have no possible future."

He shook his dark head patiently, disagreeing with her last comment. "Things can't have a future if they don't have a present."

"That sounds like a Chinese fortune cookie," she couldn't help retorting.

"There are some wise things stuffed into fortune cookies," he said lightly. She was glad he didn't take offense at her comment. He turned his head and peered out. "I think we've arrived."

The car came to a halt before a pier on Marston Lake, and they got out. Several yards away were canopied party boats with gleaming white lacquered chairs set up on their decks for the guests. On the shore were six tables laden with food. Salads molded in the shape of different animals rested on beds of ice, and were complemented by platters of cold meat. Music provided by a small band floated about the gaily decorated area.

"Nicky, darling!" came a squeal as Nick and Shane went toward the buffet. Shane looked around to see a starlet type in a silver lamé dress that looked painted on. She wiggled over to kiss Nick, then flitted on to another important person who caught her eye.

Nick cleared his throat, a trifle amused at the expression on Shane's face. "Always wondered how women could walk in clothes that tight," he said, taking her elbow.

"Her type slithers, I expect," Shane commented dryly. Nick's warm laugh encircled her.

His warm laugh was practically all she had of Nick that evening as she watched one woman after another come up to him and fawn. To his credit, she had to admit that although he seemed to like their attention, he appeared unaffected by it all. Was it that he was used to this kind of attention, or perhaps, as she hoped, he really didn't care about it? Shane scribbled down the thought on a cocktail napkin. At least she had come up with one printable observation today, she told herself.

"Is that some sort of code?" Nick's deep voice asked. She glanced up to see him looking over her shoulder at the napkin she was about to tuck into her purse.

"Just notes," she said casually. "I am working, you know."

"You have terrible handwriting."

She shrugged. "I can read it . . . most of the time," she admitted, smiling up at him. "What, no worshipful lady on your heels?" she asked in amusement.

"Dance with me, vixen," he said, then took her into his arms without waiting for her answer.

"Yes, sir," she said, saluting smartly.

"I take it you're bored."

"I've spent more interesting evenings."

"I'll see what I can do to liven things up for you," he said, whispering into her hair. It set off a series of vibrations that touched every part of her.

"Do you think you'll be able to tear yourself away?" she asked, nodding at the women around them who eyed her enviously.

"This is just typical Hollywood party stuff. Doesn't mean a thing," he said.

"Uh-oh, here comes another groupie."

"Rock stars have groupies. I have admirers," he corrected.

"You seem to have more than that," she commented wryly.

"We'll pretend we don't see her," he said, whirling her around past several dancing couples. But there was another eager-looking starlet on the other side. With smiling grace, Shane took her hands from Nick's and allowed the woman to cut in. She looked on quietly as the starlet smiled appealingly into Nick's face, her throaty laugh filling the air. Nick must have said something amusing like "hello," Shane decided.

"Hi, I've been watching you."

Shane looked around to see Miles Donovan, Nick's costar. He was not quite as tall as Nick and lacked a good deal of his presence, but he could be termed handsome nonetheless. The expression on his face made her think of someone's cocky younger brother. She imagined it must be hard to be in Nick's shadow, even for one picture.

Shane extended her hand. "I'm—"

"Shane McCallister. Yes, I know. I make a point of finding things out," he said. "So, how do you like it so far?" he asked, gesturing toward the milling people. "It's a little tame for me," he confided, "but then, this isn't Hollywood, or Vail, for that matter, so you make do," he said philosophically, downing his drink quickly and taking another glass from a passing waiter's tray.

"You go to many parties?" Shane asked, not really interested. By and large, she found small talk boring, even though it was a necessary evil in her line of work.

"As many as I can find. That's how you get yourself known. Best parts come out of knowing the right people. I met Nick at a party, although he's a devil of a person to be in the same movie with," Miles told her, his brown eyes intent on her over the rim of his glass.

"Oh?" Shane asked, warming to the subject. Maybe this malcontent would supply the chink in Nick's armor for her.

"Sure," Miles comfirmed impatiently. He sounded as if he had had more that just a couple of drinks, she thought. "All the women always flock to him and he gets all the best parts. But he's not all that good. I figure my day will come. I'm just as good as he is," he said, jutting out his square chin. "Actually, better," he said with a leering wink.

"I'm sure you are," Shane muttered. What she needed was a graceful way to extricate herself.

"Hey, how about dinner tomorrow night?" Miles asked suddenly. "I'll let you interview me."

"Thank you very much, but I only do one interview at a time," she told him, trying to walk away. He made a grab for her arm.

"Here," he said, shoving a piece of paper at her. "Here's my number. Should you find old Nick, there, is too busy frolicking to say anything to you, this is where you can reach me." He pressed the paper into her palm. "Any time."

Shane took it, promising to call if she had the opportunity. Anything to get rid of him.

Nick came up just then and rescued her, Miles almost slinking away. "He annoying you?" Nick asked, nodding toward Miles.

"No, he's just trying to make himself known," she answered.

"Not with you, he's not," Nick said. Shane felt a rosy glow spread through her at the sound of those words—despite all her best attempts not to.

The rest of the evening was a haze of faces and bits and pieces of conversations for Shane. Except for Miles, she did not find anyone who had a bad word for Nick. Everyone seemed to like him. It was getting to be a very large club, she thought, as she curled up sleepily next to him in the limousine on their return trip to her hotel. To her surprise, Nick did not ask to come in, but left her at her door with a tender kiss lingering on her lips. She felt somewhat let down as she closed the door behind her.

Sunday turned into an empty, barren day. There were no calls from Nick, no roguish figure appearing at an ungodly hour in her doorway, no plans typed in on the schedule. Nothing. Shane spent it restlessly trying to regroup her thoughts on paper and ran into an incredible case of writer's block, a malady she had once claimed did not exist.

By Monday morning, some of her spirit was back. She told herself that she had gotten carried away with the aura that hung about Nick Rutledge and had allowed herself to be swept up in the so-called legend. She almost had herself convinced by the time she reached the set, but then she saw him again and her careful facade began to crumble away bit by bit. He stood in the middle of the makeshift set, listening to the director give him last-minute instructions. He looked tired. She sat on a director's chair and wondered if some late-night tryst had taken its toll on him. She felt a harsh pain and reminded herself firmly that her curiosity was strictly professional!

He caught her eye and came over to her. "Been keeping late hours?" she asked casually.

He dropped into the folding chair next to hers, his long frame stretching out before him. "Yesterday was an incredibly long day," he said.

"Oh? Tell me about it. I'm all ears," she said with a slight edge to her voice.

He seemed to catch it as he looked at her, then grinned, his teeth a stunning contrast to his olive complexion. "And they're a shade of green."

Shane bristled. "What are you talking about? I'm merely—"

"—jealous," he said, ending her sentence for her.

"You're too full of yourself."

"Your eyes are flashing," he said.

"It's the lighting," she retorted, gesturing at the giant storklike fixtures that surrounded them as they sat in what was to be the interior of the castle. "It makes everything look like it's flashing. I've only known you for three days. What makes you presume—?"

"Chemistry," he told her, again not letting her finish. "I can feel it."

"Will you let me finish a sentence?" she cried.

"Not when I can read your mind."

She drew herself up, utterly frustrated. "If you could read my mind, I think you'd be in for a big shock right about now," she said, trying to leave. She hadn't given any thought to where she was going to go once she took her initial steps. That would come later.

But she never got to take her initial steps, as Nick's hand gripped her wrist. "Can't you take a little teasing?" he asked. "Or did I strike a nerve?" The question was asked in a very low and sensuous tone. Shane sat back down, but she made no response.

"As it happens," he said, "I had to take a quick flight out at 7:00 A.M. Seems the studio heads wanted to hold court and I, for one, don't believe in trying to buck their authority."

"From what I hear, that's a refreshing change from the usual star complex," Shane said, hiding behind her notebook as she took further notes. She knew he didn't owe her an explanation, but she was relieved and glad he was giving her one— and that it didn't include another woman.

"They pay me to do a job. If I didn't like the job, I wouldn't take it. I see no point in signing a contract and then putting on airs," he said.

His voice rang with sincerity and self-confidence. Until she had met him, she had thought she possessed a great deal of self-confidence, and it smoothed the bumpy road of life. But she had the sinking feeling she could not travel through life so easily anymore.

"Speaking of doing my job . . ." Nick said, suddenly getting to his feet. The director, John

Bowman, was gesturing for him to join his female costar. "This is where I do some of my finest acting."

Shane blinked. It wasn't like Nick to boast, and she was curious about what the scene entailed. "What do you mean?" she asked forthrightly.

"This is the scene in which I make love to my costar, a very nasty and unlovable lady in real life," he said in a stage whisper. He gave her no time to comment, turning quickly to hurry over toward Bowman and Adrienne.

Shane watched the first two takes of the scene. And she was impressed. How could he look so amorous with someone he professed to dislike? She knew he was an actor, but it was hard for her to believe that he could playact feelings so opposite to his real ones. Didn't he get any kick from those sensual embraces? And the kisses looked too real. Shane decided that anyone who married an actor was crazy—unless the actor accepted only character roles and never came within lip range of actresses like Adrienne Avery.

On the third take, with the heavy emotion of so-called make-believe passion charging the air, Shane rose from her chair. She went in search of unoccupied crew members to ply with questions about Nick.

She never looked back.

But the answers she got here took on the same hues of admiration as those she'd gotten at Saturday's party. Everyone genuinely liked Nick. There wasn't a bad word to be offered by any of them. Several of the old-timers, the people he had kept with him since the first movie, bent Shane's ear with story after story about Nick. She began to fear that readers would fall asleep reading her article.

When the cast broke for lunch, Shane took it upon herself to try to corner John Bowman. The director was not known for his patience or his gentle manner. In his time, he had sent many an actress off the set in tears, and many an actor had threatened him with physical harm. John Bowman thrived on it.

"I don't have time to waste talking to a gossip columnist," Bowman snapped as she entered his trailer.

Shane kept on coming anyway. "Magazine writer," she corrected him. "Mind if I sit?"

"Yes!"

"Fine, thank you," she said, sitting down on one of the two chairs in the trailer. She glanced about quickly. It looked like a monk's cell.

"I don't like distractions," Bowman rasped, as if reading her mind. "The only thing in my life while I'm on a picture is that picture. Now, what is it?" he demanded, lighting up a rather foul-smelling cigar, one of the two he allowed himself each day.

"I'd like your opinion of Nick Rutledge," Shane said simply, fishing out her tape recorder and turning it on. Her bag fell with a thud beneath it.

"Turn that thing off," Bowman ordered. "If you can't remember what I tell you, you shouldn't be in this business." She did as he bid her. "Nick's a man's man," he told her flatly. "I know all you ladies have palpitations each time you see him," he said, waving his hand dismissively in her direction. Shane bit her tongue and swallowed a retort. "But for all that, he's a rugged, honest, high-principled human being. None of this 'god complex' garbage that plagues so many of those fly-by-night jerks we have in Hollywood. They happen overnight and disappear that way too. Nick's going to be around for a long, long time. Comes early, knows his lines, stays out of trouble. If he thinks a scene should be played differently, he comes and tells me so. No grandstanding."

Shane tried not to cough as wreaths of cigar smoke floated her way. Her eyes smarted a little. "Isn't it true that actors are generally overgrown, insecure children, just pretending, acting out lives that they don't have the nerve to live out on their own?" Shane prodded, thinking of all the preconceived opinions she had formed before she had ever met Nick.

"I don't have time for that psychology junk. Some of them deserve to have the stuffing knocked out of them—but Nick's not one of them. I worked with him on his first picture, and I'm working with him now. There's no difference—except that he's gotten better." Bowman rose abruptly, unfolding his long, lanky frame. "That's all I have time for," he told her. "You can go." It sounded like a command. He was definitely a man used to being obeyed, Shane thought, gathering her things and shoving them into her purse before slinging it over her shoulder.

She thanked the director and made her exit. As she swung the door shut, the shoulder strap of her bag caught on the doorknob. Her momentum was such that it threw her off balance, and she tripped down the three steps leading away from Bowman's trailer. Shane was spared the embarrassment of finding herself sprawled on the ground by two strong arms that encircled her just before she landed.

"I thought you didn't fall at men's feet," Nick teased, pulling her upright.

Shane felt the warm waves of raw desire wash over her as he held her close against his body. He was still wearing the costume she had first met him in, enhancing the picture of an irresistible rogue.

"Not by choice," she murmured. She had meant the words to be a flippant retort, but instead they gave testimony to the ambivalent feelings that were beginning to pull at her.

Nick merely smiled, as if sensing what she was struggling to hide. "Old John throw you out?" he asked, nodding toward the director's trailer.

Why was he still holding her? And why couldn't she think clearly? Right now she was more conscious of the imprint of each one of his fingers upon her body than she was of anything else. "Actually, no," she said between dry lips. "He did spare me a few words. Thinks rather highly of you. Are you going to hold onto me all day?"

"The thought had crossed my mind," he said, and grinned. He purposely slid his hands in a languid motion down to her waist, brushing briefly against her hips before he freed her.

The man could retire from acting and become rich just teaching his technique with women, she thought, trying hard to recover.

"C'mon, I'll buy you lunch," he offered.

"Last of the big-time spenders," she bantered back, knowing that no one paid for meals on the set during location shooting.

Nick laughed and put his arm about her shoulders as they walked to the makeshift commissary.

The next day was practically the same. Shane came on the set and observed the hectic pace of the everyday work done to create a film. She interviewed several people. The crew became used to having her prowl about, asking all sorts of questions. It occurred to her that she was asking more questions than were necessary for her article. It was slowly beginning to dawn on her that she was trying to learn everything there was to know about Nick's life. Then, too, she found herself angling to be with him as much as possible. But his time was heavily taxed, divided as it was, between takes, rehearsals, and conferences. When he did have a spare moment, Nick usually spent it on the set rather than in his trailer, making himself visible and mingling with the crew. Shane began to see why everyone practically doted on him. He sounded too good to be true, and despite her best efforts, she realized she was falling in love with him.

And then, on Wednesday, a very strange thing happened. After lunch, Nick disappeared. She had seen him rehearsing a scene just before noon. Several people had demanded his attention when the scene ended, so Shane had gone to get a light lunch. When she returned with her tray, hoping to eat with Nick, he was nowhere in sight. She didn't think much of it until she actually went to look for him an hour later. Questioning several people who might have seen him brought her nothing but casual shrugs. No one questioned his absence.

But Shane did.

"Where did you go yesterday?" Shane asked, cornering Nick in his trailer the next morning. The makeup man was putting the finishing strokes on Nick's face, highlighting his best features. Shane sat back, leaning against a table as she watched. She saw Nick looking at her out of the corner of his eye, trying to keep his head immobile until the makeup man was through.

"I had some business to take care of," he told her vaguely.

"Oh?" Her interest was piqued by his evasive tone. "And that was?" she prodded.

"A secret," he answered in a firm tone of voice.

The makeup man chose that moment to flip off the protective cloth from Nick's neck and make his retreat. Shane was left in the suddenly silent room chewing on her pencil and eyeing Nick curiously. Up to now, he had been forthright, open. Was this "secret" the angle she was searching for? Or was Nick just being playful? Somehow, judging from his expression, she didn't think he was teasing her. He had been involved in something yesterday that he didn't want to talk about. Shane was going to find out what.

"How's the article going?" Nick asked, swinging his chair around to look at her.

"So far, if they were giving out Superman awards, you'd be the top contender," she told him glibly.

"You don't sound very happy about that," he observed, coming up next to her.

"Cataloging a person's virtues makes for very dull reading," she said honestly, trying not to pay attention to the fact that his body was almost touching hers.

"Am I dull?"

No, he certainly wasn't that, she thought. Dull was the last word she would have used to describe him. Maybe if she tried to capture his sensuality on paper, that would be enough. Maybe—

Her thoughts went no further as they gave way to a font of churning emotions. Nick's fingers were slowly weaving their way about her waist, tilting her body toward his as he lowered his head.

"I'll mess your makeup," she protested. The absurdity of her comment hit her, and she began to giggle.

"First time I ever had a woman laugh in my face," Nick said, releasing her. Someone else, Shane guessed, would have been offended. But Nick merely looked amused, as if he were thoroughly enjoying everything about her.

"First time I ever had to worry about a man's makeup," she rejoined.

"Oh?" he asked, hugging her to him. The affectionate movement surprised her. There was a definite warmth to it that went beyond that of a man merely intent on seduction. "And how many men have there been?"

She looked up into his face, drinking in every wonderful feature. "Far fewer men than there have been women for you," she countered.

"Then you must be *very* lonely," he said. There was just a touch of seriousness to his voice.

Shane laughed. "Now, *that* you can't expect me to believe." She cocked her head. "You had a zillion women throwing themselves at you at that party we went to. And that was just one night."

"That is exactly the problem," he told her. "They want to be with me for who I am supposed to be—a glamorous movie star, someone who can further their career. They don't want to be with me because they like me." He looked into her eyes. "Do you see the difference?" He made it sound important that she did.

As she studied him, she saw a well of loneliness within his eyes. This was something she had not even considered before. Could it be that even though Nick possessed a life-style people fantasized about, in reality he was lonely? As lonely, perhaps, as she in her fast-paced, career-oriented world? She felt an intense tenderness toward him as she touched his face, her cool fingers sliding slowly over his cheek.

"Yes," she said softly, "I do see the difference. And I can't understand why any woman in her right mind would think of using you to further her career when she's with you."

Nick kissed her fingertips as they passed by his lips. Good Lord, how she could love this man!

Just then, a sharp knock on the door broke the mood within the trailer. "Mr. Bowman wants you on the set, Mr. Rutledge," came the polite call.

"I could start being temperamental," Nick suggested, whispering the words into her ear as he lightly licked the lobe.

Shane shivered, but tried to keep her tone light. "What, and ruin a wonderful legend?" she scoffed. "Go out, your public awaits."

"My public," he said, kissing his fingertips and pressing them to her lips, "gets in the way on occasion."

With that, he left. Shane's heart pounded in her ears.

## *Six*

"Camping?" Shane cried in disbelief. The Saturday sun was just struggling to illuminate her hotel room as she stood, staring at Nick, wondering if she was hearing him correctly. "Why in heaven's name would you want to go camping?"

"Because I like it," he said.

He certainly looked the part of an outdoorsman, she thought. He had woken her up—again. Nick was wearing faded jeans. A blue-and-gray, half-opened plaid shirt peeked out from a denim jacket.

"Camping?" she repeated incredulously. "As in dirt and bugs and lumpy rocks?"

"Camping, as in the stars winking brilliantly over you and the earth pillowing your head," he amended. There was an amused twinkle in his eyes that Shane barely caught as she sighed, pulling the sash tighter on her robe. Stoically she made her way toward her closet and began shoving the hangers apart, searching for the appropriate clothes.

"They should have sent you someone from *National Geographic*," she muttered audibly, fishing out a peach blouse and a pair of jeans she had meant to wear only while she was working in the hotel room.

Nick sat on the corner of her rumpled bed, watching her. "We're not going to the heart of darkest Africa," he said. "Just to Rocky Mountain National Park."

"Do they have bears in this park?" she asked, refusing to take another step toward the bathroom. The clothes dangled from her fingers as she thought in horror of the prospect of running into wild animals.

"Probably," he replied nonchalantly. Then added, "You'd better get a move on. The pilot's waiting for us."

"Pilot? What are we going to do, parachute in?" Her eyes were wide with horror.

He came up to her then, putting his arms about her waist. "No." He laughed. "Not this time."

"Don't tell me, you sky dive."

"I used to. The studio doesn't approve of that while I'm filming." The clothes she held between them were getting squashed, and a warm, hazy feeling was spreading through her veins as he pulled her even closer.

"Thank God for the studio," she said, genuinely relieved. "Why would you want to take such risks?" Jumping out of planes was an activity reserved for soldiers and crazy people, as far as she was concerned.

"To experience life at its fullest," he said simply.

"That's a good way to experience death at its fullest too," she retorted, keenly aware of his face being so close to her own. She fought the urge to stand up on her tiptoes and kiss him.

He laughed again. It was a delicious laugh, which almost curled her toes in their fluffy pink slippers. "Where's your spirit of adventure?" he asked.

"I use mine up traveling on the subway every day. I see all the wild life there that I want to, thank you." For a moment, there was silence as Nick's laughter melted away and they stared at each other. He was going to kiss her, her senses telegraphed the message urgently. And as much as she wanted him to, she made a motion to separate them. She couldn't afford to get herself any more emotionally entangled than she was. An affair would be easy, but she felt that this was more than just infatuation. All she could foresee were problems and heartaches, loving a man like this.

"Um, the pilot," she reminded him. "He's waiting anxiously, remember?"

"So am I," she heard Nick murmur as she went off to the bathroom to change.

Scottie drove them to a small airstrip, where an Apache four-seater airplane stood waiting. Shane cast an apprehensive glance at the plane. She had never been up in anything but large commercial planes. She licked her lips nervously. "Don't these things crash a lot?"

"No. Once is about enough." He was obviously struggling to wipe the smile from his lips.

"Very funny," Shane muttered, wrestling with

the backpack that Nick had provided for her. The bulky object with sleeping bag attached seemed at war with her shoulder bag. She looked up to see both Nick and the pilot watching her. "I'm not good at juggling things," she snapped, hating to be caught at a disadvantage.

"Oh, I'd say you were pretty good at it," Nick told her, lifting her load and slinging it over his left shoulder. In his right hand, he held onto his own backpack, managing both easily.

Shane looked at him for a moment, trying to figure out just what he meant by his comment and deciding that it was best to leave the topic alone. She resolutely followed him to the plane, glancing wistfully at the Mercedes that was pulling away.

Nick caught her look. "C'mon," he urged, nudging her along with his elbow. "It'll be fun."

Shane had her doubts about that.

Shane had never been to a national park. The closest she had ever come was to look down at patches of green as she flew over them, going from one destination to another. Grudgingly, she had to admit that the sight of nature close up was rather breathtaking. Warm autumn colors of gold, orange, and brown greeted her as Nick helped her out of the small plane.

"Beautiful, isn't it?" Nick asked, as if reading her mind.

She nodded. The next thing she knew, he was placing the pack on her back, and she had all she could do to keep her balance. The beauty of nature was quickly forgotten.

"Thanks, Jake," Nick said to the pilot, who was already climbing back into his plane. "We'll go it alone from here."

"We will, huh?" Shane muttered, glancing at their surroundings. The area seemed lonely and desolate. She felt uneasiness take hold of her.

Nick turned back and caught her expression as the airplane taxied away. "I thought reporters were supposed to be fearless." He winked at her.

"We are, we are," she affirmed. "We just prefer being somewhere where we have nothing to fear."

"Not to worry. I'm here to protect you." He took her hand as if to guarantee the promise.

"Why doesn't that make me feel any better?" she asked dryly. Then she sighed, resigned to her fate. "Okay, Daniel Boone, where to now?"

"Down this trail here," Nick said, pointing in a direction where Shane saw no trail at all. "I know a good stream where we can set up camp and catch some fish for dinner."

"Terrific," Shane muttered.

"Spoken like a true trooper." Nick grinned. "Let's go," he urged, and with that, began leading the way.

The pack was beginning to weigh a ton already as the straps dug into her suede jacket. She wondered if the jacket would ever be the same again. She wondered if she would ever be the same again after this weekend. The fact that Nick knew where he was going astounded her. She knew that there were people who could lead you out of the heart of darkest Africa and what have you, but to her that was unreal. She had trouble going from one place to another unless the streets were clearly marked or she had a map that detailed every step of the way. Here every tree looked like every other. She knew that the sun supposedly rose in the east and set in the west, but now all it was doing was filtering through tall branches of trees, and as far as she was concerned, that didn't help one bit, other than give a charming appeal to the area.

Shane watched both sides of the wooded area apprehensively, waiting for wildlife to spring out at her. Why couldn't Nick be the type who liked to lounge in front of a fireplace with a martini in his hand the way all Hollywood types were supposed to? she wondered, staring at his back as she tried to march behind him. No, then he wouldn't be so special, she realized . . . and she wouldn't be experiencing all these dangerous feelings that she was trying desperately to keep under control.

A loud rustling noise overhead made Shane jerk her eyes toward its source, sucking in her breath. But it was only a large, brilliant blue bird flapping its wings against the dying leaves of a maple tree. A number of leaves fell down around her, and as Shane pulled her head away, she missed her footing and slid down the incline right into Nick, knocking him down. Within a moment, they were a tangle of arms, legs, and backpacks. Shane heard something go "crack" and stared down in horror at her legs.

They were both broken, she just knew it.

"You're not supposed to slide down the hill," Nick told her, getting up first and taking her hand. She made no move to accept it. "What's the matter?"

"My legs," she said, still staring down. "I think I broke them."

Concerned, Nick bent down, gingerly touching

first one and then the other. "Does this hurt?" he asked, his fingers gently exploring both regions.

"No," she said, her lips thinning. It didn't hurt. What she was feeling was the warm, stirring response of desire awakened at his touch. She watched as his fingers came closer to her groin area. "Maybe they're not broken," she said hurriedly, putting her hand on his shoulder and trying to stand up. "But I did hear a cracking noise," she told him.

"A dried branch you stepped on?" he asked, arching a brow.

She was about to agree with his explanation when she hoisted her purse and heard an unfamiliar clanking noise. Closer inspection of the contents told her that her tape recorder was no longer a whole, but a mass of parts.

"It's broken," she lamented. Shane looked accusingly at the large rock beneath her purse.

"I'll buy you a new one," Nick promised.

"What am I supposed to do in the meantime?" she asked, closing the flap on her bag in utter annoyance.

"Enjoy yourself," he suggested, beginning to walk again.

Shane took a step to follow, then winced. A groan escaped her lips.

"Now what?" Nick asked, turning around again.

"I think it's my ankle," she answered. Tiny pinpricks of pain radiated from her right ankle. "I think I twisted it."

"Small wonder," Nick said, forcing her to sit down on the rock that had murdered her tape recorder. He proceeded to pull off her intricately hand-tooled boot. "These aren't sensible camping boots," he informed her.

"I wasn't planning on camping, sensibly or otherwise, when I bought them," she retorted. She watched as he carefully rotated her ankle. It was painful, but not unbearable. "Now what? Do you shoot me?"

He laughed. "Looks fine to me," he said, replacing her boot. For a moment he stroked her leg, then rose suddenly. "It all looks fine to me," he said, his eyes meeting hers significantly.

She ignored his comment. Putting her hand in his, she got back on her feet. "How much farther to this Mecca of yours?"

"We're almost there," he said.

"A likely story," she muttered under her breath as she gingerly tested her foot. It ached just a little. "Lead on," she instructed.

"There" turned out to be a tree-lined lake with a huge waterfall at one end as a backdrop. Its waters cascaded down onto a pattern of rocks and let out into an area surrounded with the last flowers of summer. The flowers vied for space amid the newly fallen leaves that covered the ground like a multicolored patchwork quilt. Shane imagined that the Garden of Eden must have looked this way in early fall.

And here she was with Adam, she thought, glancing at Nick. Not another soul was in sight. It made her feel romantic—and uneasy at the same time.

"Was it worth it?" Nick asked.

"Yes," she said quietly. "It's worth it."

He looked at her curiously. She realized that from her tone it was obvious that she wasn't just talking about the trek to the stream. And she wasn't. Somewhere along the line, she had unconsciously decided that she should savor what was to be and not weigh the consequences so heavily. A lot worse things could happen to her than having Nick Rutledge make love to her.

Yes, a small voice echoed. She could fall deeply in love. That would be much, much worse. That, she reminded herself, would be a disaster with no fairy-tale happy ending in sight.

"So what do we do now?" she asked, struggling out of the straps of her backpack. Instantly, she felt better—at least physically.

"Now," he told her, "we set up camp and start thinking about lunch."

Lunch. At the mere sound of the word, her stomach rumbled expectantly. She glanced at Nick to see if he had heard the embarrassing noise. He had. He was grinning at her. "So where is it?" she asked, bending down to open her knapsack. Nothing but a coffeepot and a frying pan greeted her, along with some miscellaneous items she didn't recognize.

"Out there," Nick told her, pointing toward the stream as he took out several pieces of what looked to Shane like a jigsaw puzzle. After a few twists of the hand and the jigsaw puzzle turned into a fishing pole. "You've got one too," Nick said, nodding toward her knapsack.

Shane looked in again. So that was what those pieces of wood were, she thought, taking them out. It took her a lot longer to put hers together, but finally she joined him, triumphantly showing off her handiwork.

"Very good," he said. "Now cast out your line and sit down next to me."

Casting was another story. The line refused, at first, even to enter the water, getting caught on an overhead branch instead. Nick disentangled her, having the good grace not to laugh out loud.

"Maybe you weren't cut out for this sort of thing," he said sympathetically.

Which was just what she needed to hear. Thus challenged, Shane did not give up until she finally got her hook in the water, not all that far from Nick's.

"There," she said smugly, burying the hilt of her fishing rod in the ground the way he did. "Never tell me I can't do anything," she said, "because I categorically refuse to recognize the word 'can't' as part of my vocabulary."

A sensuous smile played on his lips. "You can't make love to me," he said, watching her face.

She hadn't expected him to say such a thing, and after an initial hesitation, she started to laugh. "Oh, no, I'm not falling into that trap."

"Why not?" he said softly. "I have."

His breath caressed her cheek, and somehow she found herself in his arms. Raw passion sprang up as their lips met. They dropped to the ground as one, and Shane pulled him closer to her, glorying in the weight of his body against hers. His fingers raked her hair, drawing her even closer to him. His tongue explored the sweetness offered to him, and Shane tingled with excitement as she felt the quick, sensual darting motions inside her mouth. His tongue familiarized itself with her tongue, teeth, lips, just as his hands learned the contours of her body. Her jacket had long been discarded in face of the growing noonday heat, and now her blouse was parting from her skin as Nick's sensitive fingers grazed along her breast-bone, going ever lower on her burning skin.

She moved beneath him, wanting him, wanting the exquisite sensations that he was producing to grow and last forever. His mouth left hers, as it skimmed along the pulsating hollow of her throat, making her arch her back insistently toward him. She moved his hand to her breast, aching to have him touch her, to hold her, to feed this flame that glowed inside. But the ache only grew worse as his hand went inside her bra, teasing and tanta-lizing her breast. His hands moved deftly to her back to rid her of her bra. Instantly, her freed nipples hardened against the smooth skin of the palm of his hand. He fondled her breasts gently.

Fire coursed through her veins as her heart pounded harder, mingling with the beat of Nick's own. His lips ceased kissing the points of her shoulders and dipped lower, his tongue teasing the tips of her rosy nipples, making her smother a cry of ecstasy. Without thinking, she pulled his shirt, wanting him free of it, wanting his hard, warm flesh pressing against hers. She tore a but-ton lose, and it flew into the tall grass.

Nick sat up for a moment, flinging the shirt off his body in a fluid motion. "That better?" he asked.

She had no voice with which to answer, and only nodded. All her senses were filled with him as she raised her hands in supplication. Within a moment, he had her bare back down on the car-pet of grass as he covered her chest with his own.

The hot tingle of mingling flesh excited her even more, as did the path of his wandering hand. The zipper of her jeans was sliding down and Shane felt his fingertips coast softly along the waistband of her bikini underwear, pulling the elastic down farther and farther. She lifted her hips slightly as he tugged her jeans away from her buttocks.

"Your boots, milady," Nick teased in a husky voice when her jeans would yield no further. Obligingly, encased in a mist of churning emotion, she raised first one leg and then the other, enabling him to pull off her boots and then slip off her jeans. She had nothing left except the tiny lace panties. The light blue nylon material seemed to melt away in the heat of his gaze.

Nick lowered his head, reclaiming the trail he had blazed along her quivering abdomen, his tongue momentarily playing with her navel before it forged onward. Almost playfully, his passion nearly hidden save for the sounds of his heavier breathing, Nick lifted the scant material in his teeth, pulling the translucent fabric lower, away from its rightful place. His breath mingled with her throbbing skin, becoming one with it as he rained kisses along the outline. Shane dug her fingers into his hair, savoring the wild bursts of rapture exploding within the center of her being. His tongue claimed her, making her cry for more, but Nick raised himself on his elbow and once more covered her mouth with his own. The assault was a mixture of tender passion and burning desire.

Urgently, she gripped his belt and almost jerked it free, then pulled open the snap that held his jeans in place, her ardor compelling her to go on where common sense, had it been alive at that moment, would have forbidden her to go. Some inner restraint, still strangely alive in the wake of her desire, caused her to stop for a moment. Nick's strong fingers closed over her hand and guided it down farther, so that it cupped him intimately.

The breath she drew in was audible to both of them. He smiled teasingly. And then the smile was gone, replaced by a look of unbelievable tenderness. "Oh God, Shane," he murmured, pressing her close, "I've wanted you so badly." The last words were whispered into her hair, and the length of his body covered hers.

Shane welcomed his weight gladly, shifting on the grassy bed to merge better with his flesh. The heat that pulsed from him mingled with her own as she felt his hands slip down beneath her hips, pressing them into him. With more eagerness than she had ever suspected of herself, she accepted him, moaning his name as her fingers dug into his back.

A frenzy of passion seized them both, and they moved with wild beauty and great urgency. Shane felt as though she were being pulled upward into paradise. Exquisite pleasure burst through her like a towering flower in full bloom. She trembled violently, calling Nick's name. The petals of the flower reached out and covered her then, soothing all her senses as she returned to earth.

The first thing she was aware of was Nick's warm smile. "Hi," he said.

"Hi yourself," she murmured, savoring the feel of his arms and his body against hers. She felt wonderful. More wonderful than she ever had before. This was what heaven was all about—loving a man like this.

Nick hugged her and chuckled. "I think we caught a fish."

Shane blinked. The words did not penetrate. "What?"

"There," he said, pointing. Shane turned her head slightly, seeing that one of the two poles was bent and straining.

"Lunch," she acknowledged.

Nick pushed a few strands of hair away from her flushed face.

"Could I interest you in some more dessert first?" he asked mischievously.

To answer him, Shane pulled his head down to meet hers, her eager lips parted and waiting.


Lunch had faded into dinner by the time they got around to eating anything. Nick had indeed caught a fish, as did she eventually, landing it only after he had caught two more. Nick had made a campfire, and the fish sizzled on the open flame, arranged on the frying pan Shane had carried in her backpack.

"Just like in the westerns," she commented, sitting cross-legged on the ground and hungrily eating her share. She couldn't remember when she had felt so happy.

Nick sat down beside her. "Used to do this sort of thing all the time. Red Wing and I would come down every chance we'd get and camp around here," he said, a smile on his face.

"Red Wing?" she asked, curious.

"That was his tribal name. He used 'Harry' in school. Never thought of him as Harry, though. He was a full-blooded Ute. Taught me everything he knew about the forest, what signs to look for, all the things you hear about in Indian movies. It was almost as if he had some sort of unspoken communion with the forest." Nick attempted to shake the serious effect his thoughts appeared to have on him. "I met him when I was nine. He was my best friend."

"Where is he now?" Shane asked.

"In the Ute burial grounds," Nick said, his voice strangely devoid of emotion. He put aside his tin dish.

"Oh, I'm sorry," she said, reaching out to touch his hand. "What happened to him?"

"He was in my unit in Viet Nam. He wasn't as lucky as I was," Nick said, and from his tone, she could see that the discussion was over.

It began growing dark soon after that, and Shane became more and more jumpy. The night sounds were unnerving to her, and she drew closer and closer to Nick. They sat under a tree, and Nick put his arm around her.

"Nervous?" he asked.

"This isn't the kind of night life I'm used to," she told him as they heard leaves rustle around them. A terrible sound pierced the air. "What was that?"

"A screech owl."

"Good name," she commented, looking around in all directions. She swallowed hard and licked her lips, which were terribly dry. "Nick, about bears—"

"There's one sure way to keep them away," he interrupted, his tone solemn.

"How?"

"I know for a fact they never attack two in a sleeping bag."

It was a moment before his teasing words sank in. "Never, huh?"

"Nope."

"Well, don't just sit there," she said, giving him a little push in the direction of his knapsack. "Get your sleeping bag ready."

He saluted, his eyes twinkling in the firelight. "Yes, ma'am."

Soon the fear of intruding bears wasn't even a faint threat to Shane.

# *Seven*

"Now I know why you like to go camping so much," Shane said to Nick the next morning as she rolled up his sleeping bag.

He laughed, taking hold of her by the waist. He pulled her close to him and nibbled affectionately on her ear. "I will have you know, milady, that you are the very first woman I have ever had out in the wilderness, er, I mean been out camping with."

"Ha! I heard that Freudian slip!"

"Scoff if you like; it's true. Most women don't like to get their nails chipped."

His words made her look down at her own hands. The pink polish had retreated in jagged strips, and two nails were broken. "My nails," she wailed, then looked up at Nick. A smile crept onto her lips. Her nails were all dirty and broken, but dear heaven, it had been worth it.

"Sorry you came?" he asked, helping her up.

The length of his body caressed her as he gently swayed against her. "I plead the Fifth."

"Spoken like a true journalist."

"Well, I am," she said. "Otherwise, I'd have never come on this journey into the Wild Kingdom."

"How important is your work to you?" he asked, unbuttoning his shirt.

"Very," she answered, watching him. What was he up to now? "I worked long and hard to get where I am. I intend to work longer and harder."

"To get to where?" he asked casually. The shirt was discarded as he stepped out of his pants, leaving him clad in beige briefs with white piping. The sight of his trim, muscular body held her eyes captive. She couldn't seem to get her fill.

"The top," she answered distractedly. "What are you doing?" she finally asked.

"Getting ready for a morning swim," he said playfully. "Care to join me?" Without waiting for a reply, he began to open her blouse for her.

"But it's cold," she protested.

"You'll be hot soon enough," he promised with a wicked wink, tugging at the snap on her jeans.

And she was. The more Nick stripped from her, the warmer she grew, until they both locked in an embrace, clothed in nothing but passion.

"C'mon, before I forget all about the water," he said, taking her hand.

"Is this how you do it? First you make love to them and then you drown them?" she asked, eyeing the water nervously.

"No. Now, stop hanging back. Look, you can easily see the bottom. The water here is only waist-deep."

"Are you absolutely sure?" she asked nervously. The cool air raised goose bumps along her body.

His eyes raked over every inch of her body, but she was far from self-conscious. She liked the light of passion that sprang into them. "Oh, well," he said, drawing away from the stream's edge. "There are other ways to get an early-morning pick-me-up," he added, his tone only half playful.

Before Shane knew it, it was time to turn back. She found herself really sorry about leaving this idyllic place. Nick lifted her chin with his finger.

"Don't look so sad," he said. "We can come back the next chance we get."

Shane stared at him, not daring to ask the question that had sprung into her mind. Was he just talking, or did he really intend to bring her back? And if so, what did *that* mean? Did they have an unspoken understanding? Were they having a relationship, or just a pleasant weekend? Pleasant? Now, there was an understatement. The word "fantastic" didn't even begin to cover it.

"You look very serious," Nick said, looking up from his task as if he sensed her watching him. "I don't like my women frowning."

"My women," she echoed. "Sounds like a club," she said tersely, trying to be flippant but not succeeding.

He rose and put his arms about her, the gesture a warm and protective one. "A very, very exclusive club," he told her. His eyes were unfathomable. "Right now, you have the only key."

Right now, she thought. What of later? Later comes later, she told herself stoically.

"You don't believe me, do you?" he asked suddenly, helping her on with her knapsack.

"I don't like leaving myself vulnerable," she said honestly.

He turned her around to face him. "It's a curious thing about the word 'vulnerable,' " he commented. "It has no gender. It can be applied to both the male and female of the species. And," he said, no longer serious, "I'm impulsive, remember? I always know what I want, and it doesn't take me a long time to make up my mind. I wanted you from the moment I saw you. Now, let's go, before Jake gives up on us and leaves." He gave her rear a friendly slap to propel her on her way.

Shane was left to ponder the full meaning of his words in silence as she trudged up the incline after him.

Scottie met them at the airport, and the look on his face was a mixture of concern and relief. "Boy, am I glad you're back," he said before they even reached the car. He threw open the back door. "It's been crazy!"

"Start at the beginning, Scottie," Nick said patiently, tossing his knapsack as well as Shane's into the trunk. He slammed down the lid and followed Shane into the car. Scottie took the wheel.

"They're at the house, waiting for you. They've been there for hours," Scottie told him, guiding the car out of the parking lot.

"*Who* has been there for hours?" Nick asked.

"The photographers and the extras," Scottie said, the words shooting over his shoulder.

Shane stared from Nick to Scottie, trying to figure out what was going on. Obviously the mystery had been cleared up for Nick, as he closed his eyes and sighed. "The layout! I forget all about it."

"What layout?" Shane asked.

"I promised to do some promotional shots for a magazine," he explained, "as a favor to my producer on this film."

"I thought you didn't do interviews," she said in surprise.

He shook his head. "This isn't an inverview. These are just a few pictures. Step on it, Scottie," he instructed, leaning forward. "Let's see if we can smooth their ruffled feathers."

The feathers, Shane noted later, were quickly smoothed as Nick made his apologies and then went off to change into one of his costumes. Shane was left in the living room, which was littered with voluptuous women dressed in eighteenth-century gowns designed specifically, it appeared, to show off a maximum amount of cleavage. Shane tried to make the best of it, feeling suddenly scruffy in her jeans and shirt.

She didn't realize just how scruffy she felt until Nick reappeared and sat down in the midst of the women. The startlets' eyes brightened at the mere sight of the man, and to a one, they appeared to stick out their chests in his direction. Everything about the women looked gorgeous. Unconsciously, Shane reached up to pull the scarf off her head and loosen her hair. A pang of something akin to jealousy went through her. She wondered how women married to movie stars stood this sort of thing. How did they handle their insecurities, knowing that their husbands' line of work placed them in constant contact with beautiful women who were more than a little anxious to trade their affections for the next big part on the horizon?

She watched for a while, trying to force herself to observe in a detached manner and merely take notes. After all, this was a part of the daily life of this movie star she found herself in love with. But soon she decided that maybe it would be better if she withdrew and went to her hotel.

As she rose to leave, she heard Nick make some sort of excuse to the photographers. "Hey," he asked, coming up and taking hold of her arm. "Where are you going?"

"Back to the hotel," she said with a shrug. "I'm kind of hungry, and—"

"Have Scottie fix you something," he told her. "I won't be much longer," he promised. "And I don't want you to go."

Held fast by his words, Shane did as he told her, and went to look for Scottie.

Shane found it difficult to slip back into a routine when Monday rolled around. By and large, Nick did not have that much free time for her, and she saw him primarily on the set. His evenings were spent learning the next day's lines. So their intimate, shared moments occurred in his trailer, but even then time was precious. Nick was in most of the scenes in the film, and his presence was required on the set virtually all the time.

And then he disappeared again on Wednesday afternoon.

"But where does he go?" Shane asked Scottie.

He was evasive. "Nick just . . . goes, that's all," he told her, looking about, apparently in search of a direction that would take him away from Shane. They were standing near the set where a scene was being pulled together.

Shane shook her head. "Uh-uh. These disappearances of his are prearranged. Why are the only scenes that don't include him shot on Wednesday afternoons?"

"Coincidence?" Scottie suggested hopefully.

"Scottie, tell me," she implored. In the face of what had happened on the camping trip, Shane had all but forgotten how her curiosity had been aroused last Wednesday. Now that the incident had repeated itself, she was more intrigued than ever.

Scottie looked at her, his expression for once devoid of high enthusiasm. She could almost see him arguing with himself.

"Well, he likes you," he said aloud. The words brought a certain rush to her blood. "Maybe it's all right."

"Of course it's all right," Shane said encouragingly, placing her hand on his shoulder in an attempt at camaraderie.

"There's this reservation," Scottie began, his voice lowering slightly.

When he stopped for a moment, Shane asked, "At a restaurant?"

"No, it's not that kind of reservation," he said, fumbling with a buttonhole on the cardigan he was wearing. "It's an Indian reservation."

Why would he be keeping visits to a reservation a secret, unless there was something more than tourism involved? She remembered Nick's expression when he talked about Red Wing. Did it have something to do with his friend? Aloud, she asked, "Where is this reservation?"

"It's called Cherry Creek Reservation. Don't ask me any more. I don't think I should even be telling you this much," Scottie said, obviously having second thoughts about it.

"You never said a word," she told him. "Just point me to an available car and a map."

That he did do for her, and Shane sank against the striped, cloth seat of the Mustang he arranged for her to use, staring at the multicolors of the map she had fished out of the glove compartment. Finally, she located the reservation. It appeared to be only a few miles from where they were shooting. How oddly convenient, she thought, refolding the map. Several attempts later she tossed the map over her shoulder onto the backseat. It had more creases in it than it had had to begin with. Map folding had always been something that baffled her.

Shane had never seen a real reservation, so she had no idea what to expect. It was a small area, almost like a city project, she thought as she approached it, except that there were a lot more open spaces. She saw several trailers and buildings along the way and decided that her best course of action would be to make her way to an official-looking, wood-framed building that loomed at the end of the street. Maybe someone there had seen Nick.

She found an office marked "Administration" on the first floor and knocked. A soft voice told her to come in. Shane stepped inside the small room. The floorboard creaked loudly and the sound of her clicking high heels bounced back and forth between the barren walls. The pretty, olive-skinned woman behind the desk looked up from her paper work and waited for Shane to speak.

Shane offered the woman what she hoped was her most beguiling smile. "Hi," she said, extending her hand. "I'm Shane McCallister, from *Rendezvous* magazine. Nick Rutledge told me to meet him here, but he forgot to tell me just where. I wonder if you could help me."

The woman was silent for a minute, as if she were weighing Shane's statement. "He's right down the hall," she said finally, rising. "I'll show you the way to the classroom."

Classroom? As Alice said to the White Rabbit, Shane thought, this is getting curiouser and curiouser. Quietly, Shane followed the tall young woman down the poorly lit hallway.

"He arrived a little late today," the woman told Shane, "so I'm afraid you've a bit of a wait. But you can sit in the back, if there's any room left, of course." She smiled, a touch of pride becoming evident. "It's become our most popular class since Nick started teaching it. We were afraid that he'd have to stop when his new picture began. But somehow, he managed to have the location moved to Kiowa. He's done a great deal for our young people. Well, here it is," she concluded. They came to a stop before the last door, which she opened for Shane. Quietly, the woman faded back into the hallway.

Shane did not have time to think over anything the woman had said to her—she was too busy trying not to step on anyone. The floor was literally covered with students, all sitting cross-legged on the creaky, unpolished wood. Shane stood stock still near where she had entered. There was no place else to go. Every available seat was taken, and students were crammed against one another. No one even looked in her direction or acknowledged her entrance. They kept their eyes front on the teacher in rapt attention. Only the "teacher" looked surprised. But the look quickly disappeared from Nick's face, and his lecture did not skip a beat.

As Shane listened, she realized that Nick was actually teaching an acting class. The man was a source of endless surprise to her. This was the last thing she had pictured a popular actor doing in his spare time. She watched in admiration as he took two apparently very shy students and had them read a scene from *Romeo and Juliet*, working with them until they overcame their fears and began to open up to the meaning of the words. He had a gift.

"You amaze me," Shane confessed after the last student had reluctantly left. It had taken half an hour after the class was over to clear the room of eager teenagers, who had questions of all sorts for Nick. "I came here fully expecting to find a chink in your armor and I turn up a solid-gold breastplate instead." She crossed her arms before her as she watched Nick erase the lesson from the board. "Aside from throwing unsuspecting women into pools, I think your only other bad habit is that you snore."

Nick put down the eraser and turned to look at her, cocking his head. "I snore?" he asked in surprise.

She held her thumb and forefinger up, parted slightly. "Just a little."

He shook his head, coming around the desk. "Can't be. No one in my family ever snored. We're just going to have to have you over a few more times to run a controlled test on your observation," he said, putting his arms around her and nuzzling her neck. Playfully, he kissed the silken chestnut tresses against her cheek. "How about tonight?" he proposed.

She tried to resist the temptation, her mind warning her against the folly of deeper emotional involvement. "Aren't you even curious about how I got here?"

"I figure you twisted Scottie's arm, right?" he asked, letting her go. He went back to gathering up the handful of notes he had used that afternoon.

"I'm sworn to secrecy," she said, solemnly raising her right hand. "Speaking of which, why are you making such a big secret out of this? I think it's wonderful."

"I'm not doing it to be wonderful," he told her flatly. "I'm doing it because I want to contribute something and I don't want people flocking in just to ogle me. I'll meet my fans elsewhere." He shoved his notes in his back pocket and put a guiding hand on Shane's shoulder. They headed for the hallway.

They encountered the tall Indian woman Shane had met in the office. Nick shook his head. "Anne, you should have sent her back with her tail between her legs."

The woman was slightly taken aback. "Weren't you expecting her?" she asked, looking at Shane.

"I lied to her," Shane explained before Nick said anything. "I told her I was to meet you here."

"I suppose she pumped you about the contributions as well," Nick said to Anne.

"What contributions?" Shane asked, her eyes alert.

"Nothing to concern yourself with," Nick said quickly, obviously realizing his mistake. But Shane wouldn't be put off. She turned to Anne, a question shining in her eyes.

"Nick, you are being too modest," Anne said. "There is nothing wrong with letting people know how generous you are." She turned toward Shane. "If it weren't for Nick, there would be no school. It's his money that built it and his money that helps feed these kids during the year."

Nick waved his hand to stop her. "I don't want that plastered all over a national magazine," he insisted.

Shane realized that beneath the flamboyant romantic swashbuckler there existed a very private person, who did not want any acclaim for his good deeds. But this time, she thought he was wrong. Noble but wrong. "If I do 'plaster' it all over the magazine, I guarantee you that the reservation will have contributions coming in from all over the country. Don't you see, Nick?" Shane asked, impatient that it wasn't as clear to him as it was to her. Didn't he realize the power he possessed? "Anything you're interested in, hordes of women are going to want to get involved in as well. It'll make them feel closer to you."

He looked at Anne. "What do you think?"

Anne shrugged her thin shoulders. "Sounds good

to me, although I'm not too sure how the elders will feel about charity."

Shane shook her head. "It won't be charity," she insisted. "You're giving them something back in return. You're letting people experience that glow of satisfaction over doing something good and decent, helping out their fellow man. Atoning for the Little Big Horn all over again."

"That was the Sioux," Nick corrected.

"Oh, dear. So it was. Sorry, but I do think my point is valid."

Nick hugged her close, laughing. "Lady, you're something else." She loved the feel of being pressed against him. It awakened an intimate warmth within her.

"What do you say, Anne?" Nick asked. "Will you talk to the elders and ask their permission?"

The woman nodded, parting company with them at the outer door of the building. "I'll have word for you by next week," she promised.

They waved good-bye and walked toward the car Shane had borrowed.

"What made you start here?"

"After my hitch in the Army was over, I came back here to Red Wing's family. Anne was his wife," Nick explained. "I wanted to tell her everything I could remember about his last few months. So I stayed for a while. And I began to see what a crying need these people have. The government takes away their self-respect, and to a good extent the white world still won't accept them. They're almost forced to stay here, taking the stipend that the government doles out. I wanted to do something about it. When my big break came, I was in a position to start sending money back to Anne."

They came to a halt at the car. "How close are you and Anne?" Shane watched his eyes for an answer.

"We've been friends for a very long time," he said. "Does that answer your question?"

"Partially. Look," she said briskly, "I had no right asking that—"

His fingertips brushed against the hollow of her throat as he tilted her head up toward his. The kiss that followed was powerful, yet very tender.

"Does that answer the rest of it?"

"Yes," she replied in a small, breathless voice.

"Now that that's settled, let's go to my place. You can follow in your car," he said, beginning to head toward his own.

But Shane shook her head. "You've got lines to memorize," she reminded him.

"I have a theory to disprove, remember?" he said. "I don't snore!"

"We can work on that later," she replied, wishing she weren't saying it at all. "I have to start working on my article."

"Wouldn't you rather work on the real thing instead?" he offered, spreading his hands wide. "You can bring your pad and take notes this time," he said with a wink.

"Uh-uh. I can't think around you," she retorted, opening her car door. "I'll see you in the morning." She slid into her seat.

"Suit yourself," he said, and walked away.

She watched his back, sadness filling every part of her.

# *Eight*

The next day marked the beginning of October. It was also the beginning of one of the biggest storms on record in the region. Rain lashed down in sheets, ruining plans to complete outdoor shooting begun the day before.

As Shane sat quietly in the corner, watching, she saw the director's temper go from bad to worse. Filming was not going very well at all. The humidity seemed to seep into everything. At one point, when Bowman pointed to the man in charge of the Nagra sound machine, uttering the commands "Sound" and "Speed," he was rewarded with a piercing wail.

"I don't want that kind of sound!" Bowman howled, holding his head.

Take after take was ruined by tempers, tensions, and the screech of the sound machine, which had become as temperamental as several of the actors.

The weather had the opposite effect on Nick.

"Why are you grinning?" Shane asked as he came over to her. Behind him, Bowman was threatening the sound man with physical harm unless something was done about the machine.

"The rain means snow on the mountains," he told Shane, sitting down in the chair next to her. "Good skiing weather."

"Let me guess," Shane said as if bracing herself. "You ski."

"And you don't," he concluded. "That's okay. I'll teach you."

Shane sighed. "Being around you is like being in training for the Olympics."

Nick laughed, then motioned for Bowman to come over and join them. The director looked ready to walk off the set—permanently. "Hey, John, I have an idea. Why don't we get a bunch of people together and go up to Snowmass-at-Aspen after filming on Friday? Are you game for a skiing weekend?"

Bowman shrugged his pointy shoulders, dropping an ash on his white-ribbed turtleneck sweater. He flicked it away impatiently. "Sure, why not? If I'm lucky, half the cast will break legs and I can replace all of you with real actors."

"That's what I like about you, John," Nick said. "You're an old softie."

"I must be soft in the head to take this kind of abuse year in and year out." A shrill squawk filled the air, threatening to shatter glass. "Dammit, fix that thing, Johnson, before we all go deaf!" he thundered, marching back to the harassed sound man.

•　　•　　•

Friday's rains were worse, and brought disaster with them.

"Who the hell left the equipment storeroom door open?" Bowman demanded of the crew. They were all gathered before him, each trying, Shane observed, to avoid the angry man's eyes. The director's neck was growing redder by the moment as only his voice was heard on the silent set. Bowman's eyes bore into the group. "We lost three cameras and the Nagra! Now, how do you propose we get this movie finished?" he asked, his voice trembling with rage. "Do you have any idea how long it's going to take to get replacements? The studio can't have them here until Tuesday! Tuesday! Do you know what that is in dollars and cents? Probably too high a figure for any of you to count!" He paced about, practically chewing through his cigar. "Imbeciles! Cretins!"

"What's done is done, John," Nick said easily, standing on the sideline. "It's not going to change matters if you work yourself into cardiac arrest." It appeared to Shane that everyone turned to Nick in unison, as if hoping that he could placate Bowman.

"I don't have heart attacks, Rutledge, I give them!" Bowman bellowed.

Shane thought she heard someone in the back of the group say, "Amen."

"Why don't we just break early for the weekend?" Nick suggested. "An extended rest might do us all some good. The weather report says sunny skies by this afternoon. And perfect weather for next week."

"It's better be," Bowman snapped, relighting his cigar.

"Why? Are you going to sue God if it's not?"

Nick laughed, walking over and putting his arm around the older man's shoulders. Next to Nick, Bowman looked like a gnarled and aged man instead of a frightening tyrant, Shane thought, scribbling the phrase on her pad. "C'mon, John, you've been working much too hard. You need a rest too. What do you say I have Scottie pick you up and drive us all to the airport? I've already talked to a few of the other people in the crew, and they're game."

"That's their trouble. They all think this is a game. Not a brain in the lot!" Bowman complained.

"They're the best, and you know it," Nick said. Shane thought his voice sounded a bit more firm than it had a minute ago. She was surprised to see Bowman retreat slightly. "Besides," Nick continued, beckoning Shane to come closer. "I'm going to teach Shane how to ski. You don't want to miss that."

Bowman cracked one of the first smiles she had seen on his thin lips. Somehow, even his smiles looked foreboding. Shane started having second thoughts about this weekend.

Her second thoughts plagued her the remainder of the afternoon as she went to the stores surrounding the hotel and hastily purchased some appropriate skiing clothes. This assignment was going to leave her with a broken leg, she told herself as she began to pack. A broken leg as well as a broken heart, if she wasn't careful. She chewed on her lip as she transferred the newly purchased items from their boxes into her suitcase. The weekend was going to be a mistake. She and Nick would be together, and she knew she had no power to resist him. Each time he touched her, each time he kissed her, she lost a little bit more of her soul to him.

"Damn it all, McCallister," she muttered, slamming the lid shut, "don't you see there's no future in this? What kind of a romance can thrive with three thousand miles between it? The only one that's going to be happy is the airline." She entered her bathroom, pulling out the necessary items to pack. "And how are you going to go on with that brilliant career you've outlined for yourself?" she demanded of the face in the mirror, "eating out your heart, knowing that some starlet is probably pouring her body all over Nick while you're looking for the right adjective to describe some senator's dim point of view?" She threw down her toothbrush. "If you had any brains at all, you wouldn't be going this weekend. You'd stay in your room and write your damn article and work at locking Nick Rutledge out of your heart."

But half an hour later saw her sitting in the back of a taxi, heading toward Nick's house.

"Hi, what kept you?" Nick asked as he opened the door. His greeting was warm, as was the kiss he pressed on her lips. "I was beginning to think you weren't coming. Here, let me take that," he said, reaching for her suitcase.

"I almost didn't come," she told him, and he paused in the act of closing the door, to stare at her. She turned away, not wanting him to see her expression. "I'm really not looking forward to skiing."

She felt his arms go around her waist as he pulled her back against him. His breath was warm against her neck, making her shiver slightly. "That's not all we'll be doing," he told her in a low voice. The tip of his tongue lightly brushed against her ear. Shane closed her eyes for a moment, sinking against him. Why did it have to be this man? Why did she have to fall in love with a box-office god who decorated the walls of hundreds of thousands of teenage girls' bedrooms? She had heard that his weekly fan mail count was astronomical.

"Take off your jacket," he instructed, letting her go.

"Now?" she asked, thinking that he meant to make love to her. "I thought we had a plane to catch."

"This won't take long," he promised her. Shane watched him disappear into the den, wondering what he was up to. He emerged in a moment with a large box, which he thrust at her. "Here, this is for you," he said, taking the jacket out of her hands.

She tried to balance the box gracefully as she opened it. The lid fell off, soon followed by the bottom portion as Shane took out the ermine jacket that had been cradled within the sky-blue tissue paper. She stared, dumbfounded, her fingers pressing into the baby-soft fur.

"Do you like it?" Nick asked, watching her face.

"Like it?" she echoed. "It's beautiful." She stroked the white sleeve.

"Well, then, put it on," Nick urged, his voice low as he began to slip the ermine gift on her arms.

"Nick, I can't accept this," she protested, letting him put it on her nonetheless.

"Why?" he asked, peering around to look at her

face. "Are you a conservationist? I promise you, the ermines were already dead when I bought this jacket." He came around to view his handiwork. "There," he said, straightening the opening just a bit, "you look like a princess. My princess," he added.

"Nick, I—"

"Shh," he said, placing a finger to her lips. "It's yours. I can't take it back. I already threw out the tags."

Shane shook her head, running her hand lovingly over the fur. "You're making it awfully hard to resist you," she murmured.

"Then, don't try," he told her, threading his hands beneath the jacket and about her waist. Her old jacket lay forgotten on top of her suitcase.

A loud cough kept them from kissing. They both turned to see Scottie standing on the landing of the stairway. "Um, Nick, if we don't hurry—"

Nick nodded, taking Shane's hand. "—we'll miss the plane," he said, ending the sentence for Scottie. "Okay, let's go." He grabbed Shane's suitcase with his free hand.

On the plane, Shane and Nick were reunited with about twenty people from the set of *The Lord High Protector*, and the coming weekend promised to be a hectic one. Before the plane ended its short trip, Nick had promised to participate in the poker tournament planned for the weekend. Shane began to think that perhaps they wouldn't have any time together, and the thought both relieved and saddened her. Never before had she felt so confused about her life. Never before had she wanted anything so fiercely that she'd known was wrong for her from the start. And even if Nick returned her feelings, what would the end results be? She saw nothing but frustration lying ahead of her.

But Shane did not have much time for soul searching or contemplation. Nick drew her into several conversations, and before she knew it, the plane was landing and she was being hustled into a waiting car. Nick had everything prearranged.

The lodge, nestled at the foot of a mountain, was beautiful. It looked like something straight out of a Swiss travelogue. Inside, a huge, two-sided white brick fireplace stood in the center of the lounge. A large, roaring fire licked at the dark mesh screen that enclosed it. Shane scanned the rustic, comfortable-looking room.

"Where's the proverbial skiier with the broken leg?" she asked Nick suspiciously.

"Give them time." He laughed. "They only opened for the season two days ago." Behind them, the other members of the crew and cast were signing in. The air was filled with excited conversation.

"That's highly comforting. With my luck, it'll be me," she said uneasily.

"What do you mean, with your luck?" he teased. "How many people do you know have mortally lanced the heart of Nick Rutledge, international heartthrob?" he asked with a wink.

"Pretty talk," Shane said dryly, hoping there was a modicum of truth in his words, yet afraid to find out one way or the other.

"But I'm not all talk," he said, his voice husky with promise.

She found out what he meant when she went up to her room. It was also his room.

Nick closed the door quietly behind them, setting the suitcases down in the far corner. "The slopes will be crowded about now," he told her. "I thought we'd get an early start in the morning."

"Fine by me," she murmured. It would even be finer, she thought, if he forgot all about skiing. The prospect of flying pell-mell down a hill did not exactly thrill her. She envisioned herself at the bottom of the same hill, a tangle of broken arms, legs, ski poles, and skis littering the ground.

Nick drew her into his arms, kissing the top of her head. "Don't worry. I won't let anything happen to you. You'll be as safe as if you were in my arms."

"As I see it, that's not exactly safe either," she breathed. She could feel her heart beginning to beat harder as she pressed against his tall frame.

"Living dangerously can be fun," he told her, his mouth progressing from her temple to her cheek. She could feel the fire starting, consuming all her strength and resistance.

She tried to extricate herself before it was too late. "Nick, please don't," she breathed, the words getting harder and harder to manage.

To her surprise, it worked. He stopped kissing her. But he did not release her from his embrace. "You've had something on your mind for the last couple of days. What is it?"

"The article," she said evasively, trying to look away.

But he wouldn't let it go that easily. "I know you're dedicated," he told her, sitting down on the edge of the bed and pulling her down onto his lap. "But I don't think that's it. Now, tell me," he urged, his voice soft and tender.

Shane felt awkward. What if she was presuming too much? What if he just thought that this was a casual fling? He'd laugh at all these serious inner doubts she had.

As if reading her mind, Nick said, "I think I have a right to know what's bothering you."

"Why?" she asked defensively.

Nick began to play with the shell buttons on her blouse, separating them from their buttonholes one at a time. "Because, lady, if you don't realize by now that you're pretty special to me, you're not as perceptive a writer as you've led me to believe." The blouse fell away, hanging on either side of her full breasts like a parted curtain. Slowly, Nick's searching fingers began to skim over the lacy outline of her bra, purposefully gliding over the peaked tips that strained to be free.

"How special?" she asked.

"Special enough to make me want to make you a part of my life," he told her, uncinching her belt and guiding the zipper of her pants down with the tip of his forefinger.

"That's just it," she tried to tell him, struggling valiantly to keep her wits about her as her body burned. "I don't want to be just a part—"

Nick raised his eyes to her face for a moment. "Does that mean you're turning down my proposal?" he asked seriously.

"Proposal?" she gasped in astonishment.

"Well, I wasn't talking about forming a production company. Have I been misunderstanding what's been happening between us?" he asked, his hand frozen in mid-motion. "Don't you love me?" he asked huskily.

Oh, God, yes, her mind echoed. But the tone she used in replying was hesitant. "Yes. . . ."

"But?" he pressed.

She sighed. "I'm not one to tend the home fires," she told him, wishing desperately that the words would form more clearly. Where was her wondrous ability to turn a phrase? Why was she so terribly tongue-tied now, of all times in her life?

"I wasn't intending to leave you home," he told her. "I thought I'd take you with me on location." He began to tug at her slacks.

Without thinking, Shane stood up, allowing her slacks to fall to her ankles. Nick pulled her back on his lap and removed the remaining outer clothing with one motion.

"To stand around and watch you work?" Shane asked, trying to ignore the throbbing ache that was licking at every part of her.

"No," Nick said, stroking her leg, making concentric circles higher and higher on her white flesh. "To make love with me until I'm ready to die of exhaustion—and then one more time after that for good luck." He began to kiss the point of her shoulder, his tongue teasingly outlining the strap of her bra.

"But . . . I . . . like . . . my career. . . ." she protested. One strap dropped from her shoulder, soon to be joined by the other. The total descent of the cups was hindered by the hardened tips of her breasts. Nick kissed them ardently through the thin material, making it damp.

"Fine," he said, his voice thick with desire. "You can go on with it, if that's what makes you happy," he told her, his breath coming in shorter and shorter gasps. "I don't want anything to make you unhappy."

He unhooked her bra, fondling first one heavy

breast and then the other as Shane all but pressed them into his hand.

"But that'll separate us," she protested. At that moment the idea of even a short separation was agony.

"Right now the only thing separating us is a little material," he told her, shifting around and laying her on the bed. As Shane sank down against the fur comforter, Nick made short work of her panties, tantalizing her as he slid them languidly from her hips, first one side and then the other. Her hands ached to draw him near, to touch him as he was touching her.

For a moment, he sat, drinking in the sight of her body as it offered itself to him. His shirt was stripped away in seconds, followed by his boots, then his jeans. His briefs he left for Shane to manage.

"Go ahead," he coaxed, stretching out next to her on the bed.

Shane was hard pressed to say who was more excited as she felt her heart quicken and a moan escape his lips when she drew away the material from his taut stomach and trim hips. Her cool fingers kneaded his flesh, working their way to his buttocks. She felt all control fleeing from her as the ache within her grew and grew, her body aching against his demandingly.

"Things'll work out," he promised her, whispering the words against her ear before he bathed it in short, flaming kisses. "Besides, think of the exclusive story you'll have: Nick Rutledge loses his heart to efficient journalist with fantastic body."

Anything Shane might have said in the way of a reply was lost as his mouth covered hers, almost blistering it in its demands. He was drawing away her very soul, pulling it into himself, as passion took over every fiber of her body.

His weight shifted onto hers as she prepared to receive him, all other thoughts scattering in the face of this pending throbbing ecstasy.

"I love you, Shane," he murmured over and over again, his words heavy with desire.

Rhythmically, the ultimate crescendo building with increasing force, their bodies moved against each other, each leading the other to the promised paradise ahead. The final burst of power left them both breathless, sweetly tired and wrapped in each other's arms.

"Got to admit," Nick murmured against her breast as his head comfortably pillowed itself there, "this is definitely better than skiing." He raised his head to look at her, smoothing back the waves of hair from her face. The very action was loving. "Maybe I'll just forget about the snow and have my winter carnival right here."

"Your friends would miss you," she said, tracing the outline of his mouth with her fingers. She loved his mouth, so quick to smile. She loved everything about him. Was she being a fool to have the doubts she did?

"They'd miss my money at the poker games more." He laughed, sitting up. Shane watched the muscles ripple in his back as he stood up. Her eyes darted to every part of his physique, looking at the clearly defined ribbons of stomach muscles that accented his taut waist. No one had a right to be so perfectly lovely, she thought. And he wanted to be all hers.

"You'd better get some clothes on before I stop

listening to my stomach plead for nourishment and go back for second helpings of you instead," he said mischievously.

Quickly she rose from the bed, gathering up her scattered clothing, which she donned in less time than it had taken to remove, then opened her suitcase, looking for a hairbrush. She purposely avoided Nick's eyes as she went about her small tasks.

"I won't pressure you, Shane," he said quietly. "But the proposal wasn't said in the heat of the moment. I really do love you, and something can be worked out."

"What?" she asked, turning to face him.

"I don't have all the answers yet," he told her, giving her a quick kiss as he went on rebuttoning his shirt.

She wanted to believe him, believe in the happy, fairy-tale endings he seemed to specialize in. But even she knew that Hollywood marriages usually didn't work, and that was without the burden of having a wife who worked on the East Coast. It all seemed doomed before it even came into existence.

"Success doesn't mean all that much to you, does it?" Shane asked as they came into the dining room, waving to some people they recognized. Nick guided her to a cozy table for two just as an eager waiter approached with their menus.

"No, not really. It helps me go on doing what I like doing, of course. Helps me play good Samaritan when I want to, but if I fell from the top-ten list tomorrow, I wouldn't grieve over it. I've got enough put aside now to insure my way of life for a lot of years to come," he assured her. "How's the roast beef special?" he asked the waiter.

"Terrific," the gangly youth assured him.

"Fine, we'll take two. Is that all right?" he asked Shane, who nodded.

"But don't get me wrong," Nick told her after the waiter had left. "I love my work. It's a lot of fun for me."

"And I love mine," she told him. "I love the excitement of putting together a good story, making it come alive out of bits and pieces of information."

"I see," Nick said thoughtfully as the waiter arrived with the tossed green salads that came with the dinner. Any further words on the subject were tabled as Bowman weaved his way toward them through the maze of tables.

"Eat fast, Rutledge. I've got a game starting up in twenty minutes," he told him.

Nick looked at Shane. "Do you mind?"

"Mind? I was just going to ask to sit in," Shane said brightly.

"Sit in?" Bowman repeated incredulously. He scratched the white fringe about his head. "You play poker?" he asked.

"Like a pro," she replied.

"Knew there was something about this girl I liked. Bring her along, Rutledge," he commanded, then went on to speak to someone else.

Nick grinned his approval. "Shane, you sound better and better by the minute."

Shane went on eating, loving the way he looked at her.

# Nine

Shane stayed in the game as long as she could but cashed her chips in at eleven. The men at her table grumbled good-naturedly about her quitting while she was ahead, but she begged off, saying that any second she was going to fall asleep in her seat. When Nick made a move to follow suit, she shook her head.

"No need for you to quit too," she told him.

She had fully intended to wait up for him, but once her head hit the pillow, her eyes closed, and she remembered nothing further.

"Up and at 'em, woman!"

Shane's eyes flew open, then tried to bring the world into focus. The first thing that materialized was Nick, standing next to the bed, fully dressed and holding skis.

"Up and at who?" she asked, turning over on her side, away from him. Maybe if she shut her eyes really tight, he'd go away. She had absolutely no desire to attempt to learn to ski. High heels were the toughest thing she wanted to master as far as footwear went.

But Nick wouldn't be put off. He came around the bed to face her once more. "At the slopes," he said, answering her question. "Now's the best time to hit them."

"In the middle of the night?" She groaned.

"The sun's up."

"Good, go ski with the sun. I'll join you later," she muttered, burying her head under her pillow.

"You'll join me now," he insisted, unceremoniously pulling the covers down to her feet in one fluid motion.

Shane shivered as she sat up, a flimsy aqua nightgown wrapped haphazardly around her. One breast threatened to come out at any second.

"Of course," Nick offered, sitting down on the bed, "the slopes right here are even more tempting than the ones out there. . . ." His voice trailed off wickedly.

Shane ran her hands through her wayward hair. "No, I'll be up in a minute."

"So will I," he told her.

Shane took a deep breath, feeling it safer to be out in the open with him. She couldn't think straight when she was alone with him, and there was so much to be sorted out in the light of day, she told herself. She swung her long legs down onto the cold floor, completely missing the deep-pile scatter rug and hitting the icy floor. The sensation helped bring her to. She walked over to the closet to get something to wear and realized that she hadn't even unpacked anything yet.

"Give me a minute," she pleaded, taking a fresh pullover and a pair of ski pants out of her suitcase.

"Need any help changing?" he asked as she went toward the bathroom.

"I'll manage," she promised. Somehow, she muttered to herself, I've got to manage.


"If I break anything—" Shane threatened, not at all happy about being mounted on skis. Dawn was just beginning to give light to a sleeping white world. The sun peeked over the mountains, which shimmered, silver-white, in the distance. The freshly fallen snow looked almost like newly whipped cream, with waves and peaks waiting to be touched by the first eager skier.

"I'll carry you in my arms until you heal," Nick promised as he handed her her poles. "Now, let's get started."

And so began a very long morning. He had her on the small, beginner's slope. But to Shane the hill looked enormous. She spent most of the time brushing snow off her rear. Finally, after three hours of struggling to her feet, Shane gave up. "I'm no egotist," she said, taking the hand he offered her as she got up. "I'm not going to pretend I'm going to master this sport when I haven't got a prayer."

"That's okay, Shane; there are some things you do that you've mastered very, very well." He tried to lean over and kiss her, but the skis got in the way.

"See, I told you skiing wasn't any good." Shane

laughed. "How about lunch?" she suggested. "Falling down makes me hungry."

"You're on," Nick said. "Race you down the slope."

She groaned. "I was planning on having lunch *today*," she protested.

But Nick just laughed, goading her on. Reluctantly she pointed her skis toward the bottom of the hill and maneuvered them as best she could.

Mercifully, right after lunch, Bowman demanded a rematch and Nick was drawn into another poker game. This time Shane declined to sit in, saying she had to catch up on her work. She also had to find some liniment. Her whole body was beginning to ache. She dreaded thinking about what tomorrow would bring.

Tomorrow brought all the sharp pains she had feared it would. After a night of wondrous lovemaking, she awoke in Nick's arms to find that her body felt as if rigor mortis had set in.

"Oh, Lord," she groaned when nothing wanted to move right.

"What?" Nick asked, waking up. The sound of her troubled voice brought an alerted look into his eyes.

"I'm going to die. No, change that. I think I did die. Nothing's working except my mouth. That's the only part I didn't fall on yesterday." She tried to flex her fingers, which had spent three hours tightly clutched about her poles. Every movement brought a flash of agony through her thighs.

"Everything seemed to be working well last night," Nick said teasingly, then changed his tone when he saw that she truly was miserable. "Is there anything I can do for you?"

"Notify my parents where the funeral will be held," she said, closing her eyes. Muscles were aching that she hadn't even known she had.

"What you need is a good massage," he told her, getting out of bed. She watched him throw a short robe over his nude body.

"What I need," she said, "is a bullet to bite on—and never to see another ski as long as I live." A cold wave of air tickled every part of her as Nick threw aside the covers. She heard him rubbing his hands, working liniment into them. Then she felt him lift her nightgown up to her shoulders.

The feel of his hands upon her back brought a bittersweet agony to her. "Relax," he told her, "relax." After a few minutes of kneading, Shane's moans of anguish subsided. "All better?" Nick asked.

"Well, it's actually my legs that are unbearably sore." She immediately realized her mistake.

Nick poured additional liniment all over her upper thighs and began to rub it in. He gently spread her legs apart.

"What are you doing?" she cried.

"You want me to be able to massage your entire leg and get you moving again, don't you?" she heard him ask innocently

"Now I know why you like to give skiing lessons. It's the day after you're really interested in."

"Not true," Nick replied. "Let's just say it's the scenery I like," he quipped. It took Shane a few seconds to catch his meaning, and then Nick had to duck a flying pillow. Shane moaned in pain.

"Serves you right," he chided, getting back to his task.

While his hands worked away her soreness, Shane's mind drifted off. The man was wonderful. How could she hope to maintain a relationship, much less a marriage, with a man who was even better than hearsay purported him to be? No, she'd be much better off not allowing herself the luxury of making plans for the future. If she just thought of this as a romantic interlude, maybe someday she could handle the emptiness that would surely come.

"Hey, are you falling asleep?"

Nick's voice drifted into her stream of consciousness, and she shook her head, or tried to. "Oh," she cried.

"What's the matter?"

"My neck. . . ."

"I'll get to it," he promised. "There're just so many lovely details to keep me occupied below your neck," he told her brightly, his fingers fanning out from the region just below her shoulder blades. His palms pressed on either side of her spine as his fingers reached out farther and farther, getting closer to the tender flesh of her breasts.

And then all she was aware of was the delicious sensation of his touch on her breasts. "It doesn't hurt there," she murmured, smiling.

"I want to keep everything in absolute tip-top shape," he replied, "especially something I value so highly."

Shane tried to draw herself up on her elbow and failed. Nick pushed her head back down.

"I'm not finished."

"Would you have paid any attention to me if I were flat-chested?" Shane asked, disturbed by his comment.

His hands slipped beneath her breasts, cupping each one as he bent over and kissed the nape of her neck. "Lady, I would have paid attention to you if you were flat-chested, toothless, and losing your hair. It just would have taken me a little longer, that's all. After all," he said, turning her over to look at her face—and other parts. She saw the look of desire in his eyes as they slid over her body. Her nightgown was still tucked beneath her arms. "After all, visual aids do count for something. Look at me," he ordered, sitting down next to her. "I know that if it weren't for this face, I wouldn't be where I am today. I'm not overly talented, just very, very lucky. If I looked like this," he said, twisting his lips and pushing his nose over to one side with his forefinger, "I might be on the docks somewhere, unloading freight—and no one would know how wonderful I was inside," and he grinned, then stretched out next to Shane.

"Oh, they'd know," she assured him, raising her arms to him. He enveloped her in a warm embrace, his body resting familiarly next to hers. "Somehow that magic that's you would come through—you'd earn enough money to have plastic surgery and wind up looking just the way you do now, the fantasy of millions of women."

"I don't care about millions of women," he said, his eyes not quite as merry as they'd been a moment ago. "They're just attracted to the cosmetic part, the part I have no control over. I care about a woman of judgment—someone who can see beyond that," he explained, kissing her neck, bringing about a new surge of excitement to her. "I want to be part of *her* fantasies." The kisses trailed up Shane's chin, coming to a climax on her lips.

The remaining aches her body felt melted away in the heat of her rising passion.

"Nick, I'm too sore to go on the slopes today," Shane protested as Nick drew her out of bed nearly an hour later.

"I just checked out everything," he informed her, pushing her toward the shower stall, "and it's all in working order, lubed, and ready to go," he added with a chuckle.

As soon as he withdrew his hand from the small of her back, Shane stopped moving, digging her toes in the throw rug to keep steadfast. "Yesterday was a disaster," she reminded him.

"So," he said, patting her rear, propelling her two steps on her way, "today's got to be better."

"Want to bet?" she asked, crossing her arms before her and turning defiantly in his direction.

Nick walked in ahead of her and turned on the water in the blue-tiled bathroom. He tested the temperature, then took hold of Shane's hand and pulled her toward him. "Talk about stubborn women," he muttered playfully, stripping the nightgown off her. It floated like a cloud down to her feet. "When you fall off a horse, you're supposed to climb right back up."

"Fine," she said. "Find me a horse and I'll do it."

There was no arguing with him, so she gave up and went into the shower. The cold water made her yap in surprise. "You're trying to kill me," she accused, above the sound of the running water.

"Just trying to revitalize you," Nick said.

She looked back at his shimmering form, separated from her by the frosted glass of the shower stall. That, she thought, he had done very well only minutes ago. Silently she quickly scrubbed her body, trying not to think of the pains that were returning.

Nick was still leaning against the sink when she emerged a few moments later. There was no mistaking the glow of approval in his eyes. "Here, let me," he said, taking the fluffy blue bath towel from her hands. With long, deliberate strokes, he dried her glistening body, rounding each curve slowly.

She tried to stand perfectly still, knowing he was teasing her. And she tried her best not to respond. She had more of a chance of becoming an Olympic skier overnight, she decided, wrapping her fingers in his thick dark hair as he bent his head. The strokes on her thighs felt more like caresses.

"You're driving me crazy," she said between gritted teeth.

"Good"—he laughed—"because the feeling is mutual." He rose off his knees. "Now, be a good girl and get dressed," he ordered, "before I change my mind and decide to keep you prisoner here all day."

That, Shane thought, struggling to raise her aching legs in order to get into her clothes, would be far preferable to facing another skiing lesson.

In the dining area, Shane and Nick were surrounded by several of the crew members. "What say we have that tournament, Nick?" one of the men suggested.

Shane was all for that. Anything to forgo having to mount skis again. She knew that since everyone wanted to win, no one would chose her for his side, and she'd be safe. At least, that was what she thought.

"But I *can't* ski," she protested vigorously when Nick chose her for his team.

"It's not going to be just skiing," Nick assured her.

"Terrific," she muttered into her coffee. "Just how many ways are there to break your bones up here?"

"That's what I like about you," Nick said, patting her hand. "You're so game to try everything."

"It's not that," Shane complained as he took her by the arm and pulled her along after the departing crowd. A sea of ski jackets marched before them. "I just thought I'd reach the end of the month in one piece, ending this assignment with all the parts I had when I came into it."

But that wasn't strictly true either, she thought as Nick turned for a moment and gave her a strange, warm look. She didn't have all the parts she'd started out with. She didn't have her heart.

"I don't know how to toboggan either," Shane informed Nick as he stood at the crest of a small hill, pointing to the people he'd chosen for the first event. Shane eyed the toboggan skeptically.

"You know how to sit, don't you?" he asked.

"Yes, but—"

"That's all you have to do," he told her. "The toboggan does the rest."

She had her doubts that it was all that simple,

but found it useless to argue. She allowed herself to be plunked down on the oversized sled, sitting right behind Nick.

"Wrap your legs on either side of me," he instructed, turning his head slightly so that she might hear above the noise.

"So that's why you chose me," she said, enlightened.

"Never miss a chance," he told her. "Everybody ready?" he called over his shoulder.

A cheer went up to tell him that they were.

"Okay, Benny, push!" he ordered, and Shane felt the toboggan tilt slightly, bending into the wind.

The rush of cold air licked greedily at her face, and she buried it against Nick's back, wrapping her arms around him tightly and holding on for dear life. She had to admit that she liked the roller-coaster effect the ride had on the pit of her stomach. It felt strangely like the plummeting feeling she experienced when she and Nick made love.

The other team won.

"Rematch!" Nick hooted, cupping either side of his mouth with his black, fur-lined gloves. "I demand a rematch!" Amid groans and laughter, everyone trudged up the hill once more. Somehow, it looked a lot bigger this time than it had at first.

The process was repeated again.

And again.

"Enough!" cried the captain of the other team. "We win, and there'll be no more rematches!" Cheers and muffled applause met his announcement. Some of it came from Nick's side.

A skiing event was next, and this time Shane

was allowed to stand on the sidelines and merely cheer her team on, which she did to the utmost of her ability. She found herself almost going hoarse as she watched Nick and the other team captain come barreling down the hill, masterfully maneuvering their skis past the obstacles that had been set up.

She held her breath as Nick took a near spill, but he recovered himself in time. He went on to win the event. Swept away by the mood of the crowd, Shane clapped wildly, despite her aching arms.

Nick skied over to her. Impulsively, she kissed him.

"Remind me to win more often," he joked. He sounded slightly winded. "Help me off with these, please, I want to watch Pete," he told her, referring to another member of his team.

"You're going to be a hard act to follow," Shane said, doing as he asked.

"I'm counting on it." Shane looked up at him, not at all sure he was talking about the skiing competition. But his proud bronze head was turned from her. Shane kept her thoughts to herself as she rose to join him.

The small but boisterous ranks of *The Lord High Protector* cast dominated the slopes all morning and part of the afternoon. A large crowd of spectators gathered once word had spread that they were there. Tourists and serious skiers alike came to watch Nick Rutledge in action. Whenever his form wasn't flying down the slopes, he was besieged by fans with requests for autographs and pictures. Shane watched quietly as she saw him comply with each request for an autograph, smiling genially. She wondered if the mob of fans realized how sharply it was cutting into his privacy.

The combined strain of competing and being mobbed by fans soon took its toll on Nick. She could see that he was growing tired. She turned to Scottie, who had joined her in Nick's absence. "C'mon," she told him, taking his hand, "I think your fearless leader needs rescuing."

"What are you going to do?" he asked, allowing himself to be woven into the growing throng of people encircling Nick.

"Follow my lead," she instructed, then raised her voice, trying to sound very official. "Thank you very much for coming, folks!" she said, straining her voice to be heard above the din.

Nick looked quizzically in her direction. He was standing with his arm around a heavyset giggling woman. Her royal-blue ski jacket made her look even wider than she was, and Shane wondered how Nick managed to get his arm all the way around.

Shane pushed her way forward, clearing the crowd away from Nick. "Mr. Rutledge has to be getting back now. He's in the middle of filming, and this is all the time he has for a break."

Protests greeted her words, but no one pressed to get any more pictures. Members of the crowd began to drift away, until Nick was able to follow Shane and Scottie out past the perimeter of the group.

"Very resourceful," Nick whispered, going down the slope and toward the lodge.

"It looked as if you were going to be stuck all day," Shane observed. "And you're too polite to tell them to get lost."

"That's rather harsh," Nick commented. "I'd never want them to get lost . . . just disappear for a bit now and then."

"Is it always like this for you?" she asked as he pulled open the huge, ornately carved door for her and held it while she and Scottie walked in.

"No, usually it's much worse," he confessed. "At least I got one day of quiet out of it. In this business you learn to be thankful for that."

"Life in a goldfish bowl."

"Something like that," Nick said. "Puts a strain on you at times."

"You seem to be bearing up well," she said as they made their way into the dining hall. A sea of heads turned toward them.

"I found a nice tranquilizer," he said, the words spoken softly against her cheek.

"Uh-oh, here comes the second wave," Scottie warned. Shane and Nick turned on their heels and left quickly, deciding to rely on room service for their dinner.

# Ten

They left early the next morning, before conditions at the lodge became difficult. As it was, Shane was awakened at three in the morning by someone at the door who refused to go away until Nick gave her his autograph.

"I think you need a bodyguard at your door," Shane had suggested sleepily when Nick returned to bed.

"Tell you what," he said, sliding in close to her. Somewhere between the floor and the covers, Shane noticed that Nick had managed to shed his pajama bottoms again. "You guard my body for me tonight," he proposed, with a fresh sparkle in his eyes.

Shane did more than guard it.

But the idea of a bodyguard did sound like a good one to her as they all but sneaked out of the lodge the next morning, trying to avoid being noticed. Nick's world certainly did have its draw-backs, she thought as she snuggled close to him in the taxi bound for the airport. And it all went part and parcel with the man. She wondered if she could cope with it all and whether she could stand being part of the background if she gave up her career for him.

A new problem met them on their return to the set. Nick had only meant to stop by to pick up his copy of the script, which he had left in his trailer. Bowman apparently had preceded him to the set, and could be heard bellowing at some cowering gofer who had delivered a message.

"Sounds like all our little vacation did was im-prove John's voice," Nick said in a loud "aside" to Shane as they approached the director. The set was empty, and their words sounded strangely hollow, echoing about the cardboard interior of the Saxon castle that was Nick's home in the movie. "What's the trouble, John? The studio re-route the cameras to Hawaii?"

Bowman looked at Nick, disgust written over his lined brow. The gofer took the opportunity to retreat from the line of fire. Shane stood qui-etly by, paying minimal attention to the scene, cocooned in the ermine jacket Nick had given her. Her thoughts were on her own problems.

"No, the damned cameras are on their way," he snapped.

"So? Why the sunny smile?" Nick prodded.

"It's that damned girl!" Bowman rasped, chew-ing on still another cigar. He slapped his pockets for a match and came up empty. "Got a match?" he demanded of both of them.

Shane shook her head.

"Filthy habit, John," Nick told him. "If you don't give it up, you'll only live to be ninety instead of a hundred." Bowman thrust the unlit cigar back in his shirt pocket. "What damned girl?" Nick asked casually. He leaned against the long stairway where his big dueling scene was to take place. The look on his face was patient.

"The short one—the one with the hair . . ." he muttered, once more searching his pockets for a match.

"We don't have any actresses who are bald, John," Nick reminded him. "At least not to my knowledge."

"The one who did all the shampoo commercials," Bowman spat out in exasperation. His search had been useless as well.

"Oh, Mona. What about her?"

"She's down with hepatitis," Bowman said accusingly, as if it had happened merely to annoy him. "And we were set to shoot first thing tomorrow. Blast it, where the hell am I going to get a replacement now?" He ran his hand over the short white fuzz that covered the top of his head.

Nick was quiet for a moment, and Shane caught him staring at her closely. The light that came into his eyes made her uneasy. When he had talked about his love for his profession on the flight back, she had mentioned to him that she had been in several productions in college. She had admitted to liking the sound of the applause when the final curtain came down. She could see now that Nick was connecting the two pieces of information.

"Shane has Mona's coloring," he told Bowman.

"So does the wardrobe mistress," Shane pointed out, shaking her head in protest.

"Too old and too short," Nick said. He turned to Bowman. "What do you think?" Shane thought he sounded eager.

Bowman circled her, frowning deeply. Shane felt almost like an inanimate object. "If anyone asks me, I think it's crazy," she retorted. Bowman kept circling slowly. "Mr. Bowman, there isn't that much of me to see. Please stop circling like that."

"Might work," Bowman said to Nick. "Might work. It's not a big part. Can you memorize lines?" he snapped at Shane, addressing her for the first time.

"Yes, I can memorize lines, but—" Her protest went unnoticed.

"Okay," Bowman announced. "What do we have to lose? We'll try her. You, give her your script," he said to Nick. "Tell her what she has to do. And you," he ordered, pointing a bony finger at Shane, "get your tail down to wardrobe early tomorrow. You look like what's-her-name's size, but she's flatter than you. Wardrobe's going to have to adjust something or other." With that, he stomped off, muttering something about wishing he'd never gotten into the movie business in the first place.

Nick put his arm about Shane's shoulders. "Welcome to stardom."

Shane blinked. "What just happened here?" she asked, still a little shell-shocked.

"Old John worked his charm on you," Nick told her as they walked out into the bright daylight again.

"I don't think this is such a hot idea."

"You'll be terrific," Nick assured her, kissing her temple. "Trust me—I have an instinct about these things."

"Oh? Is that what you say to all the young starlets who flock to you?" she asked coyly as they finally rounded the corner to his trailer. Nick unlocked the door.

"Only the ones who make me absolutely wild! Don't worry, it'll be fun. I'll be right back," he promised, slipping out of sight behind the door.

Shane leaned against the trailer, crossing her arms over her chest. Fun? Well . . . maybe . . . just a little. A smile began to form on her lips. It would be an interesting angle to include in her article. Why not? It'd be a lark. And hadn't she once wondered what she'd look like in a movie? Hadn't every woman in a dark theater given way to such daydreams at least once?

"All set," Nick assured her, coming down the two steps from his trailer. He took her hand. "C'mon, let's get started. I'll be your coach," he said, hustling her back to his car.

Shane spent the night with Nick, learning her lines and movements for the three short scenes that were to be hers. The flavor of the movie became more evident to her, and she actually found herself enjoying the make-believe world that was being created. And she began to understand Nick a little better too.

Nick's command to rise and shine seemed to come five minutes after she had put her head down on the pillow. Before she even had a chance to open her eyes, Nick was throwing off the covers and pulling her out of bed. No morning light seeped through the heavily draped windows. Shane tried to focus on the luminous dial of the antique clock on his bureau.

"Nick, it's the middle of the night," she cried.

"No it's not," he told her, pulling her into the bathroom.

"My mother taught me that 4:00 A.M. comes in the middle of the night," she protested.

"You've got an early call at the wardrobe department," he reminded her, shedding her nightgown for her, then stripping out of his pajama bottoms.

"What are you doing?" she asked.

"I thought we'd shower together," he told her with a grin. "Saves time."

It very nearly didn't, not with his soaping her body the way he did. For vengeance, she returned the favor, making sure she took an extra-long time lathering him. She could feel his response to her. She smiled triumphantly, turning her head as he tried to kiss her beneath the water streaming from the shower head.

"Uh-uh," she said, wagging a finger at him. "Remember, I have an early call—"

"And I have an early urge," he replied, shutting off the water and pulling her into his arms.

"Nick! You up?" Scottie's voice came through the closed outer door as he knocked several times. "I'll have the car around front to drive you to the set in five minutes," he announced.

Shane felt Nick's body sag in defeat against her. "I shouldn't have promised his mother I'd look out for him. So far, he's interrupted us three times." He threw open the shower door and grabbed at the towel first, holding it out of Shane's reach. She let her hand drop, waiting.

"If you were a gentleman, you'd let me have the towel first," she said, pretending to pout.

"Oh, I'm a gentleman, all right. But I also like seeing your body glistening with water, the beads shimmering all along the length of you. They make very interesting patterns that I'd like to trace when time permits," he said, allowing his finger to follow one path along her breast, down her nipple, and then along her rib cage to her navel.

"The studio," Shane reminded him with an effort, taking up the smaller, hand towel and beginning to rub herself dry. If she let him continue, all the words she had hammered into her head last night would vanish in the flames of her passion.

"Good waist," the wardrobe mistress pronounced as she adjusted the heavy, beaded gown to Shane's body. Shane was to play the daughter of the king, and as such had three different, beautiful gowns to wear. This was the ultimate little-girl fantasy, Shane thought, trying very hard to hold still and not perspire under the weight of the dress.

"Healthy bosom, too," the older woman said, nodding as she let out a seam right under Shane's bust. "Good cleavage for the camera."

They made it all sound so technical, Shane thought. It was almost as if she were reciting numbers out of a catalog.

"There," the woman muttered, smoothing out the wide white lace collar that accented the décolletage of the dress, "that should do nicely. Pretty color for you, too," she added, pleased with herself. The dress was a deep green brocade, with white beads woven all through it. The lower part of the sleeves hung to the ground. "Better hurry along, dearie. Mr. Bowman hates to be kept waiting," the wardrobe mistress advised her, practically waving her on her way.

As if she could hurry anywhere, Shane thought. Trying to maneuver in the dress was tantamount to learning how to ride a bike. She lifted her hem and tried to point herself in the right direction. The dress grew heavier with each step she took toward the set.

She arrived just in time to catch the end of the director's speech informing everyone that he fully intended to make up for any time they had lost due to the ruined equipment. He had never had a picture run over its allotted time, and he didn't intend to start now.

"Not much of a pep talk, is it?" Nick whispered, coming around behind Shane. She looked up at him in surprise, not having expected him to pop up like that.

He looked more surprised than she did. Or was the word "pleased"? she wondered, watching him take in the picture that she made in her stunning costume. She was afraid to move her head too quickly, for fear of dislodging the tiny crown that perched atop it. To cut down on time, the wardrobe mistress had sent for the makeup artist, and Shane's makeup and hairdo had been taken care of at the same time. Shane was ready to go as soon as Bowman called on her, and now she stood eyeing him nervously. What had she gotten herself into?

"You're the most beautiful princess I've ever seen," Nick said as the crew members began to take their places behind the scenes. "But don't look so worried."

"I'm not," she lied. The butterflies in her stomach were turning into jumbo jets.

"Glad to hear that." Nick adjusted the cape that hung rakishly over one shoulder. "But I think you've gone pale under your makeup," he pointed out mischievously, casting a sly glance at her.

"It's just this costume," Shena complained. "It's a wonder women in those days could even more."

"That's why there was so much hanky-panky going on," he whispered. "The ladies couldn't run away."

"I'll buy that. But how did they sit?" she asked with a moan. The dress felt stiff and unwieldy, standing out on either side of her small waist like a huge growth.

"They didn't. They went straight to a lying-down position." He looked at her longingly for a moment, or so she thought. It made her forget her discomfort for a fraction of a second. "But if you're really tired, there's a special chair set up for you over there." Nick pointed off to the side.

Shane saw what amounted to a cushioned version of a slanted board with armrests. "What?" she asked, thinking he had made a mistake.

"That," he said, nodding. "Keeps you from wrinkling your costume."

"Looks like a theme and variation on a torture rack," she commented, eyeing it suspiciously.

He drew her over toward it, then positioned her carefully, tilting her body just a little, so that her shoulder blades rested against the cushion first. Her long string of white pearls sank down against her chest as she did so. "See, it's not so bad."

It wasn't. What was bad was trying to get out of it. She couldn't stand up without help. Nick did not have the good grace to hide his amusement as he pulled her upright again.

"Tell Bowman I want more money," she said high-handedly. She could feel a bead of perspiration sliding down her back, trailing into the heavy material of the gown. And she wasn't even under the hot lights yet!

"An actress for five minutes, and already she's getting temperamental," Nick said to a passing extra, who grinned back.

"Let's go, people! This film isn't going to make itself—although it'd probably be a damned sight better if it did!" Bowman yelled, waving in annoyance toward Nick and Shane.

"Uh-oh," Shane said in a very small voice.

"What's the matter?" Nick asked, whispering the words against her ear as he ushered her forward.

"I think I have to go to the bathroom."

"Just nerves," he assured her.

She was going to be terrible, she just knew it.

The cry of "Action!" echoed in her brain, mixing in with all the lines of dialogue she had tried so hard to memorize the night before. Carefully, trying not to look at the camera, which was a few inches away, or so it seemed, she pretended she was the character she was portraying. Shane turned from the huge tower window that supposedly looked down on the courtyard, and "gasped" to find Nick staggering into her "room."

"Shh," Nick cautioned, putting a finger to her lips. "I am a friend."

How could a person act with lights and cameras all around? she wondered, trying to keep her attention strictly on Nick. "Friends do not sneak into ladies' chambers," she said, drawing away from him. Nick had rehearsed her to take two steps backward and look up. Sure enough, a "cord" that was to summon the royal guard hung there.

Nick's hand was over hers. "Pray, stay your hand for but a moment and hear me out. I would restore the rightful king to his throne. Pull that cord, and it is not only my head that will be on your conscience, but that of the king as well, and all of England will rue your deed."

"The king?" Shane echoed, beginning to enjoy herself. "You are a friend of my father?"

"Truly," he said with a bow. "And I would be your friend as well." He came toward her, his hand lightly caressing her cheek. "I had no idea his daughter had grown into such a flower of loveliness."

The movements he used were ones Shane was very familiar with, and she wondered where the actor ended and the man began. He drew her into his arms, and Shane prayed that the wires beneath her gown would not swing out at him.

"We should not be alone like this," she murmured. And suddenly she did feel alone with him, alone amid a score of crew members, whirling cameras, and a scowling director. How many other actresses had felt this way with Nick and would feel this way with him in the future?

"Yea, but we should," Nick whispered audibly, and he kissed her. The kiss felt like all his kisses did. There was no acting here, no fine line drawn between the world of reality and the world of make-believe.

"Cut!" Bowman's voice rang out in the midst of the sweetness penetrating Shane's world. "Cut, damnit! Seduce her on your own time, Rutledge!"

That drew a laugh from the crew, and Shane blushed slightly as Nick drew back his head. He kept his arms about her.

"How about it?" Nick asked, nuzzling her hair.

"Is that how you end all your scenes?" Shane couldn't help but ask. She kept a smile on her face but didn't feel one inside. What she felt inside was nagging uncertainty. Could she overcome these doubts?

"Only with my female costars," he told her with a wink. Then he grew serious as hairdressers emerged out of the shadows, studying both of them carefully to make sure that every hair was in place before they reshot the scene. "Hey, is that a note of jealousy I detect?"

"Not jealousy," she denied quickly, then added, in a lower tone, "maybe just a little insecurity."

"Insecurity? You? The cocky journalist who goes where angels fear to tread? The lady who beat John Bowman out of a hundred dollars at poker?" Nick threw back his head and laughed. His hairdresser stared daggers at him before combing down a lock of hair that had fallen into his eyes. "You're the last person in the world who should feel insecure—about anything," he told her firmly, reaching out and squeezing her hand.

She smiled back at him, telling herself that she was being foolish. But the nagging little voice stayed with her until late that evening, while she was working on her article. Only then did it fade away. She realized that she needed her work, needed her identity, in order to show up phantom fears for what they were—baseless apparitions.

"Not bad." Bowman nodded on the second day of shooting. "Considering you're a rank amateur, that really wasn't half bad."

"Heady praise from a hard taskmaster," Nick told her dryly.

"None of your lip, Rutledge," Bowman snapped. "Let's take it from the top!"

Cameras began to roll again.

Shane's presence on the set was required for only three days' shooting. This included reshooting the one scene that the actress she was replacing had already completed. When it was all over, Shane was a little sorry that it had ended so quickly. Nick was right. It was fun, despite all the hassles, the makeup, which made her itch, and the uncomfortable positions she had to assume while waiting for her next scene. It was hard work, but enjoyable.

"There'll always be a part for you in one of my pictures," Nick told her as they drove to the reservation the following Wednesday.

"Have I become part of your entourage?" she asked glibly, smiling, allowing herself to pretend for just a moment that there could be a "happily ever after" for them. "I heard that you tend to keep a lot of the people who work with you."

"You may add new meaning to the word 'keep.' "

She knew he had meant the words as a joke, but they cut nonetheless. Even within this whirlwind of emotion and passion she was experiencing, she knew that she couldn't give up everything for Nick. They both would be miserable eventually if she were just Mrs. Nick Rutledge, submerged within his lifestyle.

She caught him looking at her intently when she made no response to his comment, and she wondered if he knew what she was thinking. He seemed so tremendously intuitive about things that concerned her.

They rode the rest of the way with Nick making pleasant small talk. For once Shane was glad to lose herself in meaningless conversation.

# Eleven

Everyone was waiting for Nick.

"Got a full house again," Shane whispered as he parted from her in back of the room. She watched him as he went to the front of the class. The sounds of chattering voices melted away in his presence.

This time she found a place to sit on the floor and flipped open her notebook. She knew that Nick wasn't keen on her writing about this aspect of his life, but it was too good an opportunity to pass up. She wanted her article to do more than just join the ranks of the others that had gone before it, listing sweet, love-struck platitudes about his wonderful eyes and fantastic profile. She wanted readers to see *why* this man was special— not because he could swing from a masthead and save the "fair heroine," but because he was a man who cared and gave of himself.

Shane felt her heart bursting with love and despair at the same time.

"You hold them in the palm of your hand," she commented after the class was over.

"That he does."

They both looked up to see Anne entering the room. She looked very pleased. "The elders said yes," she told Shane without any preamble. Shane had nearly forgotten that Nick had stipulated they get the council of elders' permission before she mentioned anything about the reservation. She thought about her notes and felt a pang of remorse. In her eagerness for a good article, she had been as guilty of ignoring the tribe's privacy as Nick's fans had been at Aspen. Shane hoped that Nick did not notice the fact that she flushed. Damn her complexion anyway.

"That's wonderful," she said quickly, jotting a few things down for their benefit. She had already taken all the notes she needed during Nick's lecture. "This will really work out well for everyone in the long run," she promised.

"Not to mention our little writer, here," Nick said affectionately. "Well, I'll see you next week, Anne."

Anne nodded. "For your final class."

Shane looked from the slender Indian woman to Nick. "It's over?"

"Afraid so. I can only get the filming done here for so long. We have to go back to the studio to do most of the interior shots," he explained.

Shane shook her head as they left. "Don't you ever get tired of being so noble?" she asked. Nick opened the car door for her, and she slid in, wishing the car didn't have bucket seats. She wanted to curl up next to him. Next week might not be just the end of his class. It might mark the end of their relationship as well. He hadn't mentioned marriage since that time in the lodge. Perhaps he was having second thoughts on the subject as well. She didn't doubt that all the problems of a bi-coastal marriage were becoming more evident to him as well.

"Yes, I get tired of being noble," he said, taking hold of the wheel. "Let's go to my place and I'll do something shamelessly *un*noble. I'll make love to you from the minute we enter the house until first call tomorrow."

"Trying out for Superman next?" she asked drolly.

"No, vixen, just trying to satiate my enormous appetite when it comes to you." His gray eyes made love to her, and she felt warm all over. "So far, all I've managed to do is whet it."

"I thought you had that big scene coming up tomorrow," Shane said, remembering something she had overheard earlier that day.

"I do."

"Shouldn't you be studying your lines, then?"

"I should. But I don't always do what I should—and I'd rather study your lines," he added with a leer.

She knew she should decline, knew that the longer she allowed herself to wander through this wondrous world of make-believe, the harder it would be for her when the final break came, but she just couldn't help herself. She wanted to be with him every moment she could.

"I suppose I might ask you some more questions for the article," she said slowly. Dusk was descending all around them, and Shane stared straight ahead as Nick flipped on the headlights. It was a lonely, isolated area, and no other cars passed them along the way. Lonely. The word sounded horribly foreboding.

"Good, I've already told Scottie to set another place for dinner."

"You knew I was coming all the time!" she accused.

"How could you resist me? Hey, hey, don't hit the driver," he cautioned. "Unless you want to run us off the road and leave us stranded here all night."

She could think of worse things, but let her hand drop back in her lap.

Any plans they might have formed for the evening ahead were set forcibly aside when they arrived at Nick's house.

"Now what?" Nick asked as he opened Shane's door for her.

She was going to miss all his gallantry. She was going to miss *him*. "What's the matter?" she asked, suddenly realizing that Nick was frowning hard.

"Our director." He gestured toward Bowman's beloved 1958 Corvette, which was parked at an angle in the driveway. "Never did learn how to drive," Nick commented, shaking his head. "I wonder what he wants."

When Nick walked through the huge white double doors, the director almost sprang at him.

"What were you doing, hiding behind the door?" Nick wanted to know, shutting it behind Shane.

"I've been waiting for you!" the director said

accusingly. "Why don't you keep decent hours, like normal people?"

"There's nothing indecent about five-thirty, John. What's the matter, somebody steal the film?"

"Don't get smart, Rutledge. Here." The older man shoved a stack of pages into Nick's hands.

"What's this?"

"Tomorrow's scene."

"But I have tomorrow's scene," Nick reminded him.

"You *thought* you had tomorrow's scene," Bowman corrected. "I had that idiot of a screenwriter rework it. Now it sounds like something!" he said triumphantly. "Oh, hello, McCallister," he said, as if noticing her for the first time. Curtly, he nodded in her direction. Shane forced a quicksilver smile to her lips, which faded the next moment.

"Well, get to it. You're on call at eight sharp. Be there!" he warned, despite the fact that Nick prided himself on never being late for anything, much less a call.

Bowman barked something as he departed, and slammed the door behind him. Nick looked up from the pages he was thumbing through. "That man will never win the Miss Congeniality award."

"Wrong sex," Shane pointed out.

"Wrong temperament," Nick corrected. "The other part can be overlooked." He dropped the pages on the marble-top table that stood against the wall in the foyer. "On to dinner."

Shane stood her ground. "Nope," she informed him, picking up the script and handing it back to Nick. "You study. I'll go home and have room service take care of my needs."

"I didn't know room service provided *that* kind

of service," he said archly, accepting the script from her nonetheless.

"Food, Nick, food. Where's Scottie?" she asked, looking around the large, stone-tiled area. "He can drive me to the hotel. I've got lots to keep me busy tonight," she assured Nick, patting her notebook.

Reluctantly, Nick called Scottie and asked him to take Shane to the Cosmopolitan.

Shane spent a productive night, revising some of her notes and writing furiously into the wee hours. Forgotten, a half-eaten, stale sandwich sat next to her. Every so often, she'd recall its existence and take a bite, not even conscious of what she was consuming. A smile spread to her face. It was shaping up quite nicely, she told herself, biting down on limp lettuce. The soda she washed it down with had long since gone flat. Shane didn't notice. Nothing mattered except the flow of the words onto paper.

Feeling extremely satisfied, she laid the article to rest at 2:00 A.M.

At five she rose again, almost as if in a dream. Nick had gotten her used to waking up early. She stretched, feeling the emptiness of the place next to her. Oh, yes, she was in her hotel room, she reminded herself. Nick had certainly gotten her used to quite a bit more than just getting up early. How quickly life can change directions, she thought, padding across the carpeted floor to the bathroom.

She stood, contemplating her dry toothbrush. How quickly was she going to get used to *not* having him around? Not very fast, she told herself with a heavy sigh. That might take her years to accomplish, she thought, squeezing the last drop of striped paste onto the bristles. She had to remember to pick up some more today. She spread her lips wide as she brushed vigorously. Mustn't offend him during the last few days they had together.

An hour and a half later found Shane shivering on the set. She was one of the first persons to arrive.

"Really getting to like this stuff, aren't you?" Bowman asked. He didn't seem surprised to find her there. He didn't even wait to hear her answer, as he began bellowing orders that made an army of power packs and electrical generators appear, marring the beautiful Colorado countryside. Shane tried to get out of the way of the cables that were snaking their way along, every which way she turned. She found it safest to follow in Bowman's tracks.

"It is kind of exciting," she admitted to the back of Bowman's head, watching the long, thin hands motion impatiently for a cameraman to come closer, "seeing the disconnected bits and pieces of film make a story."

Bowman jerked his head in her direction. "They don't always do that, you know. Sometimes all you come up with is a God-awful mess. Takes an overall vision."

Shane assumed he meant *his* vision, and kept still. She let him talk, welcoming the backdrop of sound while she scanned the area for Nick's familiar form. He was to film the chase sequence this morning, she had discovered. The script girl had allowed her to read the newly written pages over her shoulder. There was also a new love scene with Adrienne Avery. Shane had already decided not to stay around for that.

"Hi."

Just the sound of Nick's voice did wonderful things to her, she thought as she turned to face him. He held aloft a brown bag, then gave it to her.

"Peace offering. For letting me study my lines—for *making* me study my lines," he corrected.

Puzzled, she opened the heavy bag. "Pistachio nuts!" she exclaimed, looking back up. "Where did you—?"

"Had Scottie comb the local grocery stores. That's a composite of about twenty packages. They don't pack very many in those little cellophane bags," he commented, shedding his sheepskin jacket and handing it to her. "Save me some," he ordered, leaving to mount the snow-white stallion that was being used in the chase sequence.

Shane grinned, holding the jacket close to her. How like him to be so thoughtful. They had discovered a mutual passion for pistachios while at the skiing lodge. Nick had remembered that—even though his mind was filled with the millions of details of getting a part just right on the screen.

Scottie brought a chair for her, and she sank down gratefully, hanging Nick's jacket on the back as she watched him ride closer and closer, chasing Miles Donovan, who played the heavy. Every woman's hero, she thought with pride and a touch of sadness as her fingers became redder and redder, shelling one pistachio after another.

"Hey, they're almost all gone," Nick said, pretending to complain as he squatted next to her chair, his broadsword clanking on the ground.

Shane looked sheepishly down at the bag. There was hardly anything left except for the opened shells. "I'll make it up to you," she promised with a wink.

"See that you do," he ordered, slipping his jacket over his shoulders. A sudden cold breeze rustled the high grass and made Shane shiver despite the warm ermine jacket. She curled her fingers so as not to get any of the red stain on the fur pile. "I have an idea. You can come to the costume party with me this Saturday."

"Another party? Boy, you actors lead a hard life," Shane said wryly. Scottie came up and offered them both steaming-hot cups of coffee. She accepted hers gratefully.

"I'll have you know that this one is for a good cause," Nick informed her, pretending indignation. "It's for charity. And you should be thanking me."

"Oh, and why, pray tell?" she bantered.

"Because there're going to be a lot of celebrities attending," Nick told her, taking a long sip of coffee. Shane watched his Adam's apple as he swallowed. *Dummy, you're acting like a star-struck kid, trying to absorb every movement your idol makes.*

"What are they doing here?" she asked, looking around at the vast countryside.

"Not here," Nick said, gesturing at the terrain, "Aspen. This is the beginning of the skiing season, and skiing is very 'in.'"

"No accounting for taste," Shane commented. "Are we flying back up there?"

"No, they're all flying down here. It's Gloria's party."

Oh, yes, Gloria, the party giver, Shane recalled.

"Does Gloria do anything besides give parties?" Shane asked, munching on another nut.

Nick reached into the almost empty bag and took several for himself. "She backs my pictures."

"Mustn't offend Gloria," Shane quipped.

"Now you're getting the hang of it." Nick grinned. He put the empty shells in his pocket and took out another handful of nuts, cutting Shane's remaining supply in half.

"What do I do about a costume?"

"How about coming as Lady Godiva? That's simple. I'll lend you the horse—or you could ride me," he proposed with a sexy smile.

"We'd never get to the party."

"How about your costume for the film?" he suggested helpfully.

"Only if I want to spend the whole evening as a doorstop. It's pretty, but mobility is definitely not one of its advantages. No, I'll come up with something," she promised, rolling the idea around in her mind. She thought of Martha, the wardrobe mistress, and an idea began to form. "Leave it to me," she said airily.

"Rutledge, are you planning to phone in your performance?" Bowman called. "Get your butt over here!"

Shane waved gaily as Nick walked off toward the white stallion again.

Shane surveyed her reflection, a wide smile of approval on her lips. Martha had worked wonders with a minimum of effort, she thought, whirling about and watching the hot-pink material float after her. The harem-girl costume looked as provocative as anything Shane could have fantasized. Made of shimmery material that was layered discreetly, allowing just enough cover for modesty's sake, the skirt hugged the lower portion of Shane's hips invitingly, exposing a bejeweled navel.

The silver bolero jacket was deeply cut and laced together with slender threads. If she took a deep breath, she thought, it would be all over. The tips of her nipples threatened to show as they rubbed against the soft interior. She was going to have to be careful, she told herself, adjusting the gold armbands Martha had given her. Shane fastened her veil, taking care to leave her flowing hair free. Sultry. That was the word, she thought with satisfaction. Salome, eat your heart out!

It was obvious that Nick was eating his out when he first laid eyes on her. She pretended not to notice as she slid into the backseat of the limousine, trying to keep her jacket shut. But the jacket did precious little to hide the outline of her legs beneath the skirt's gauzelike material.

Nick was dressed as a Viking. A horned helmet lay next to him on the seat. He quickly pushed it to the other side, allowing Shane to move closer. "Now I know why the Vikings like to loot and pillage strange new lands. Look what they could come up with," he said in admiration. "Let's see the rest of it," he coaxed.

But Shane clutched tightly at the jacket's collar. "All in good time, my Viking lord, all in good time."

"You're turning into a real temptress," Nick said, shaking his head. But he let her have her way. Shane smiled smugly all the way to the party.

"Martha's getting risqué in her old age," Nick

said, his eyes echoing his obvious pleasure as Shane peeled off her jacket. She handed it to the very stiff, very proper butler, who also offered to take Nick's fur cape. But Nick declined. "The lady might have need of it if she inhales deeply," he commented, eyeing the thin lacing on Shane's bolero. "I should have made Scottie take us to my place," he murmured into her hair. "God, you smell good. I might need this sword just to keep men away from you all night," he teased, patting the scabbard at his side.

Shane felt all eyes upon them as they entered the huge ballroom. As at the last party, peaceful music floated through the air, thanks to a large orchestra that played off to the side. But there were many more people at this one, and Shane recognized more than a few faces that had graced movie screens across the world. Despite the fact that the room was tremendous, it was filled to capacity with gaily clad partygoers. She glanced at Nick, but he seemed to be looking for someone. Probably their hostess, Shane thought, picking out several faces she knew and making a mental note of them.

"This way, Shane," Nick said, taking her arm. "There's someone here I want you to meet." She wondered what big-name movie star or producer he was going to introduce her to. Instead he brought her over to an aging, distinguished-looking Rhett Butler. Next to him stood a very young-looking Scarlett O'Hara, making Shane once more aware of the fact that men were always interested in young, pretty women. Once a woman reached a certain age, her face became a liability, and another sweet young thing emerged to take her place. She looked at Nick, wondering how many "sweet young things" would dog his tracks ten years from now.

"Alexander Tate, I'd like you to meet Shane McCallister," Nick said, presenting her. "Shane's with *Rendezvous* magazine."

"Ah, yes," Tate said, a genuine smile touching his mouth. He raised her hand to his lips and kissed it. "I'm familiar with your work."

What an odd way to put it, Shane thought. She judged the man to be a jet-setter. Probably read *Rendezvous* while sitting in different airports around the world, waiting for his flight.

"Well, I'll leave you two to get acquainted," Nick said, suddenly leaving her side. Shane stared after him, confused. Just a moment before, he had been so attentive. What had caused this change? "Ginger?" Nick asked, offering his arm to the woman at Tate's side. "How about a quick whirl around the floor? Watch him," Nick warned Shane audibly. "He's not as harmless as he looks."

And with that, Nick and Ginger disappeared into the crowd, leaving Shane strangely feeling empty. Get used to it, McCallister. It's coming by and by. She turned to Tate and forced a smile. "He seems to have run off with your date," she said, her throat unusually dry.

"My daughter went quite willingly, I assure you."

His daughter? Shane looked at the distinguished-looking man in a new light. "So," she said, "you've read some of my articles. I'm flattered."

"You're also very good," Tate told her.

A waiter walked by with a tray of glasses filled with champagne. Tate took two and handed Shane one. As he talked and asked her questions, Shane looked over the rim of her glass, hoping to catch a glimpse of Nick.

# Twelve

Shane did her best to be polite to Tate. She tried not to be too obvious as she kept an eye out for Nick. But soon her answers to his questions were no longer preoccupied, and she turned to the man with genuine interest as he went on engaging her in conversation.

"Why don't, we sit down somewhere so we can talk without getting in the way of the traffic?" Tate suggested, taking her arm and leading her to a nook. Obviously the man knew his way around, Shane thought, and he was used to taking charge, though in a low-keyed manner. She offered no protest, wanting something to take her mind off Nick's abrupt disappearance. "Scarlett O'Hara" was quite beautiful.

Tate gestured toward an unoccupied sofa that was partially shaded by a potted palm and flanked on the other side by a large window that offered a view of the vast grounds behind the house. Guests were milling about on the terrace, which was bathed in soft, colored lights. Shane noted everything as if she were a person apart from herself. The way she felt about Nick was affecting her normally keen eye. This was going to have to stop, she told herself sternly, sitting down. She was a mature woman, not some wide-eyed, teenaged romantic.

The eyes that looked at her were keen and interested as Tate continued to ply her with questions about her work, her interests, and her political opinions. He delved into a lot of corners without being offensive. It was one of the first times Shane had talked so much about herself without learning a great deal about the person she was speaking to. Yet she found herself liking Tate and his manner. He had put her at ease almost immediately, making her feel as if she were in the company of an old family friend instead of a stranger. Maybe it was the costume, Shane thought. She had grown up loving Rhett Butler and having him fill her fantasies.

Fantasies. Where was Nick? She tried not to be too obvious as she looked past Tate's shoulder through the long green fingers of the palm, searching the crowd once more for Nick. A glimpse of white fur went by, but it was only someone dressed as a polar bear.

"He'll be back presently," Tate said warmly.

Shane flushed, embarrassed. "Your daughter's very beautiful." Now, why in heaven's name did she say that? The man would know exactly what was going on in her mind.

"And very resourceful," Tate added mildly. Terrific. Did that mean that the raven-haired woman was sewing Nick up as her own right now?

"But Nick is very taken with you," Tate said, and Shane almost dropped the goblet she was toying with. She stifled the urge to pump Tate with eager questions, asking how he knew something like that. That, she told herself, was supposedly reserved for high-school girls and long, afternoon phone conversations about the dreamboat in one's homeroom.

"He speaks quite highly of you," Tate offered when she couldn't think of a suitable response.

"Have you known him long?" she asked, wondering just what Tate's connection with Nick was. He had offered no information about himself, appearing only to be interested in what she had to say. In a subtle way, she realized, he had been questioning her.

"Since before he had his first rippling muscle," Tate told her.

"Then, you were neighbors?" she prodded.

Tate brushed a speck of dust from his cut-waist vest, which hung from his thin body. "Once," he replied without looking up.

Boy, some interviewer you are, she thought disparagingly. Can't even get full sentences out of Rhett Butler.

"Ginger's worn me out."

Shane looked to her left in surprise as Nick returned with the voluptuous Scarlett still clinging possessively to his arm. They were both laughing.

"I give her back to you," Nick said, handing her over to Tate.

"Oh, dear," the silver-haired man said, rising,

"that means I have to find someone else to occupy her for a while." He turned toward Shane, who was still seated. "Thank you, Miss McCallister. I had a very pleasant chat." He made Shane a little bow; then, offering his arm to his daughter, he left.

Nick sat down next to Shane, putting his arm about her shoulders. "Have a nice talk?" he asked.

"Yes, I guess you can say that . . ." Shane's voice trailed off.

Nick laughed. "Alexander's a little eccentric," he agreed, obviously interpreting her tone to mean that she wasn't quite sure how to take the older man. "But geniuses are allowed to be."

"Geniuses?" Shane echoed, looking at Nick quizzically. "What does he do?"

"Oh, Alexander's dabbled in a lot of things in his time," Nick said evasively. "Care to eat?"

Shane nodded, and they went in search of the sumptuous buffet that Nick had assured Shane their hostess was famous for. At the long table Shane found more gourmet foods than she could conceivably hope to sample in one evening. Absolutely everything looked tempting to her.

But the food did not hold her attention for long, as Nick began to introduce her to people she had only seen gracing the front covers of magazines or read about in newspaper articles. Names that flashed by in movie credits became flesh and blood for her as the evening wore on. Nick's life-style had its definite attractions, she thought, enjoying herself thoroughly.

Suddenly there was a hush, and the milling sea of people parted as the hostess, dressed as Guinevere, came forward.

"And now," she announced, "for our talent contest." This was met with enthusiastic applause.

Shane moved closer to Nick, looking forward to the show. "This promises to be good," she told him in a whisper. She couldn't understand why he was grinning at her so mischievously as Gloria went on to refresh people's memories about the rules of the competition. Each contestant had to do something that was connected to the costume he or she wore.

"Our first brave entry," Gloria announced, "is Miss Shane McCallister."

Shane's eyes widened in horror as she heard her name. She jerked her head sharply toward Nick.

"I volunteered you," he told her.

Her hands turned icy. "But what'll I do?" she asked in distress, between lips that could barely move.

"You're a harem girl," Nick said, pushing her slightly forward. "Dance."

The applause was kind, coaxing her to step up to the cleared area. Sultry music pervaded the air. Shane turned back to look at Nick, who smiled encouragingly. Obviously he had told Gloria that she was going to dance.

For a moment, Shane stood immobile, trying to recall a movement, a gesture with which to begin. And then her body just took over. Her hips began to sway to the tempo of the Eastern melody. Slowly Shane gave herself up to the music, her dancing becoming more and more heated. By the time the last crescendo cut through the air, Shane was dancing with controlled abandon, her cheeks glowing with exhilaration.

She returned to Nick, followed by a din of hearty applause.

"You rat," she said, slightly breathless.

Nick held up his right hand solemnly. "I cannot tell a lie—you were magnificent." He hugged her to him. "We're leaving soon," he told her, whispering the words in her ear. Someone else was performing now, but Nick's words, pregnant with promise, drew all Shane's attention.

"But the party—" she protested, although not very strongly.

"We'll make our own," he promised her, running his finger along her lips.

The thrill of anticipation took hold of her body as she snuggled closer to him, her shoulders partially draped by his fur cape.


Pins and needles of excitement coursed through her veins as she leaned against him in the dark interior of the limousine. They were going to his place. Her heart sang. And for another night, ecstasy would keep the future, with its cold realities, at bay. She willed herself not to think of anything but the warmth of his body next to hers and the thrill of his lovemaking.

Scottie let them out at the front door and took the car around to the garage. She didn't see him again until the next morning.

"Come, milady," Nick said, scooping Shane into his arms at the foot of the spiral stairway, "I wish a private performance." Shane cradled her body against his chest, the melody from the seduction scene in *Gone With The Wind* floating through her head. But Rhett Butler, she mused, never held a candle to Nick Rutledge.

He carried her into his vast bedroom and closed the door softly behind him. One lone, brass lamp gave light to the dark. Nick pushed a button over the carved headboard of his bed, and the ceiling retracted before Shane's surprised eyes. The stars she had admired on the trip back now winked at her through the domed skylight.

"Dance," Nick whispered. He sat down on the bed and watched.

Shane kicked off her shoes. The tiny bells on her ankles tinkled seductively as she began slowly to sway to the inner music she felt. This time there was no wild abandon; this time the dance was performed as a rite of love as she moved seductively closer and closer to Nick, tantalizing both of them.

She watched his face as she took off first one armband and then the other, tossing each to him with a wicked smile on her face. She wasn't even certain what possessed her to behave like this. Maybe it was the costume, or maybe it was the woman in her that Nick had awakened with his kisses. She wasn't sure. She didn't care. All she wanted was to bring out and heighten the look of love and desire she saw flickering in his eyes.

The transparent layers of her skirt came floating toward him next as she peeled them off one at a time. The process was slow and deliberate. The last layer left her in the tiniest of panties. A ribbon beckoned invitingly on either side of her hips. But she ignored that and went on to the thin laces of the shimmering silver bolero. Deftly her fingers pulled at the tiny cord, drawing it away

# LOVESWEPT

## Love Stories you'll never forget by authors you'll always remember

from the first hole, then from the second, and finally the third, leaving the material barely draping the sides of her breasts. The pink tips of her nipples peered out teasingly.

Shane heard Nick mutter an anguished groan as she drew nearer, offering herself to him and then drawing away at the last moment. The sides of her bolero hung open, exposing the fullness of her ripe breasts to his ravaging eyes. She could hear his breath quickening as she whirled slowly around the bed, thrusting her body forward and then pulling it away. The bells jingled hypnotically as she drew closer again. With calculating movements, she offered her hip to him.

Nick pulled at the pink ribbon that was there, causing it to fall open. She shifted her weight, hardly able to stand the excitement herself. Nick's fingers parted the other ribbon, and the last shred of material on her body drifted to the floor. Moonlight illuminated her nude body as Nick reached out for her.

"C'mere, you," he breathed huskily, his voice choked with emotion.

"No," she whispered back. "You're not ready yet." She breathed the words into his ear, touching his ear lightly with her tongue. She caught the involuntary shiver and smiled. "Stand up," she commanded seductively, drawing him up against the length of her body. She could feel the hard outline yearning for her. Her satisfaction deepened.

With fingers that were almost trembling, Shane unfastened the fur cape that was draped across his right shoulder and let it fall to the floor. One by one she undid the lacings of his leather vest, her

throbbing fingers caressing the hard muscle that met her touch as the vest parted. She slipped it off his shoulders, coming around behind him and taking care to allow her breasts to brush teasingly, lightly, against his back. She heard Nick whisper her name.

Nick turned to take her.

"Not now," she warned, still determined to go on. She came around to face him once more, applying herself to his leggings next, stripping away the leather lacings until his bared legs met her gaze. Rising to her feet, she found him waiting for her. But there was one more article in their way.

"Never met a Viking in briefs," she murmured, her hands slipping in on either side of the blue cotton that clung to his firm hips. His skin felt hot.

"And how many Vikings have you undressed, vixen?" Nick asked. His voice sounded strained, as if he were fighting for control.

"Just one," she replied, sliding the material off one hip and then the other with deliberate movements. The briefs fell away. Shane raised her head, pressing her body against his. "Now," she said. "Take me now," she all but pleaded, entwining her arms around his neck.

The passion that exploded within them took a long time to quell. With the stars defining their boundaries, Nick made love to Shane, not once, but several times, that night. Each time brought with it fulfillment and the sting of bittersweet sadness. Shane sought desperately to lose herself in Nick's arms, feverishly making love to him.

"Hey, what is it?" he asked at one point, his

arms cradling her as the length of his body fit against the soft contours of her own. She clung to him, her nails digging into his back, pulling him in closer to her. Nick stopped moving and pushed away the strands of hair that had fallen into her face.

"Just love me, Nick," she cried, pulling his head down closer to her, her lips yearning for his. "Just love me."

"I do," he murmured against her mouth, scorching it once more with the intensity of his kiss. One arm pillowed her head while another stroked the side of her body, stroking her over and over again before it slipped beneath her hips.

She parted her legs, responding to the signals that had become almost like second nature to her. She felt the hot, urgent thrust within her and gloried at the sensations that rushed to meet it. Their ragged breathing mingled and echoed through the dark room as the united rhythm of their movements increased, reaching up to the ultimate burst of fulfillment.

Shane prayed that something would hold back the dawn and let her die within the ecstasy created by the only man she would ever love.

The last week of her assignment passed like water through a sieve, despite the way she tried to cling to each moment. After her weekend in paradise, Shane found it harder to concentrate, harder to face the reality that she knew was waiting for her. Some women would have thought of her as the world's greatest fool, giving up a life with Nick for a career that was only partially

formed; a career she still had to work at in order to mold it into what she ultimately wanted. But she knew that in the final analysis, she wouldn't be complete unless she was her own person. And besides, she thought ruefully, Nick had never repeated his proposal, never even brought up the fact that she was supposedly considering his offer of marriage.

Shane watched Nick film still another scene as she sat in the shadows of a darkening set. It was a night scene, and the conditions were perfect. Most likely he'd regretted his proposal the minute he had made it, she thought. She wasn't going to be some pathetic, clinging vine and remind him of it. That wasn't the kind of woman he was attracted to, she told herself. What she had had was a month made in heaven. A month that had enough passion in it to last her for a lifetime.

It would have to, she thought with tears in her eyes.

The last-minute details of filming on location took up almost all of Nick's free time, so Shane was left to her own devices, and threw herself into her work. The article that emerged from her pen was the finest she had ever written. A labor of love, she thought with a sad smile as she sat in her lonely hotel room, trying hard not to relive every moment of their time together. Later she could take out those memories and explore them, handling them like fine, delicate Christmas ornaments to be cherished and preserved. But not now. Now they were still rimmed in pain. Now she had to work and be the bright, efficient woman who had breezed onto the set almost four weeks ago.

She accompanied Nick to the reservation again and took part in the small end-of-semester party that the students threw for him. She watched him closely and was delighted to see that he had as good a time at this party as he had had at Gloria's charity ball—perhaps even better.

Her time alone with Nick was limited to driving to and from the reservation because of the demands of the shooting schedule. Still, she consoled herself, she'd have the last night.

Or so she thought.

"A dinner party?" she repeated, trying to hide her dismay as he presented the idea to her that last afternoon on the set. Her plan to spend an intimate evening in his arms crumbled. Perhaps he was embarrassed to be alone with her, she thought. Perhaps he was afraid she'd raise the issue of his marriage proposal. Well, he needn't worry about that. She was adult enough to handle the situation. Still, she avoided his gaze, knowing he had the ability to see the pain that she was experiencing. Instead she watched as various crew members busied themselves with packing the equipment, getting it ready to ship back to the studio. A man Nick had introduced as the production manager was rushing around, issuing orders.

"Who's going to be there?" she asked, pretending to be interested.

"Alexander Tate and his daughter," Nick said. They began to walk back to his trailer. Shane concentrated on putting one foot in front of the other.

She glanced covertly at Nick's face. Was there a special light in his eyes when he mentioned Ginger? Or was that just her imagination? How

loving Nick had brought her into close proximity to her best and worst emotions! She would have sworn she didn't have a jealous bone in her body until meeting and falling for him. Even in her brief marriage, she hadn't experienced jealousy, so much as hurt. Grow up, McCallister, she ordered sharply. Jealousy is for fools. And besides, you haven't the right to be jealous of Nick. He hasn't made any commitment to you.

Nick was standing in front of his trailer, and she almost walked into him, oblivious to the fact that he'd halted. He put his hands on her shoulders to steady her.

"Hey, whoa, there. What are you so preoccupied with?" he asked, studying her face.

She looked away. "Just the end of my article," she lied. And the end of us, she tacked on silently.

"Work on that this afternoon. I'll have Scottie pick you up at seven. Don't be late," he said with a wink.

"I never am," she said, attempting to sound carefree.

"Amazing woman." Nick laughed, blowing her a kiss.

She pretended to catch it, then turned and walked away, her heart aching.


Nick's chef had outdone himself, Shane thought as she sat in the spacious formal dining room that evening. But she discovered that her appetite had deserted her. She wasn't the least bit tempted by the delicate dishes that were served. Shane was placed opposite Scottie and next to Tate, who sat at Nick's right hand. Ginger sat at his left.

Shane tried not to let the seating arrangement bother her.

"Nick tells me that you'll be returning to New York tomorrow," Tate said.

"Yes," Shane replied dully. Back to New York. Back to her career. Back to her life without Nick.

"Tell me, would you consider making a career move at this time in your life?" Tate asked, taking her completely by surprise.

"I beg your pardon?" She must have misunderstood him, she thought. The question came out of left field.

"Would you consider making a career move at this time?" Tate repeated, his tone as soft and unassuming as ever.

"If a good offer came," Shane said honestly. "I'd be more than willing to consider it."

"Would you consider a position as a senior writer on *In-depth* magazine a good offer?"

Her eyes grew wide as she realized that conversation had otherwise stopped at the table and now everyone seemed to be waiting for her answer. Knowledge sizzled through her like a flash of lightning.

"*In-depth* magazine?" she repeated dumbly, her mouth forming an unspoken "Oh" as the truth rushed in on her. "You're *that* Alexander Tate? The owner of *Indepth* magazine?" She hoped that the squeal she thought she uttered was only in her imagination.

"Among other things," he told her. "How about it?" he prodded. "I realize that it would mean moving from New York. I like my writers to stay close to the home office," he explained. "And the home office is in Los Angeles."

He needn't have told her that. She knew all about *In-depth* magazine. It was an even classier publication than *Rendezvous*, and the position Tate mentioned was one she would have given her eyeteeth for—if she had come by it honestly.

Shane eyed Nick suspiciously, but he merely smiled at her, appearing to be as interested in her answer as the others were. There wasn't a trace of smugness in his expression. Had he arranged all this, or was she being unduly mistrustful?

"I would consider an opportunity to work on the staff of *In-depth* a godsend," Shane said. "The move from New York would be a small price to pay for the privilege of being part of the staff of your magazine. But—"

Tate didn't seem to hear the last word. "Fine. It's all settled, then. Here's my card," he told her, fishing it out of his breast pocket and handing it to her. "Give me a call, and in private we'll discuss salary, benefits, that sort of thing. Then, of course, I'll have your contract all drawn up and ready for you to sign."

Shane stared at him, stunned. It was too good to be true, she thought. Things like this just didn't happen, except in the movies. The movies. Yes, it did smack of romanticism. It smacked of Nick.

She said nothing more on the subject for the remainder of the evening, which was short. Once Tate's "mission" was accomplished, he and his daughter did not stay on very long. Tate said something about having an early flight to catch, and he thanked Nick for a wonderful time. And for the tickets.

"Tickets?" Shane questioned as they returned from seeing their guests off in the front drive. Out

of the corner of her eye she saw Scottie making his way up the stairs, leaving the two of them alone.

"I sent him airplane tickets."

"To come here," Shane said, filling in the rest of his statement.

"To come here," he repeated, nodding.

"And offer me a job." She felt angry tears that she only half understood forming in her eyes.

"I was hoping. Hey, what's the matter?" he asked, his voice echoing slightly in the foyer. He looked utterly puzzled.

Shane shut her eyes. How could she make this come out right? "Don't you see, Nick? It doesn't mean anything if you get me the job. I have to get it. I don't believe in favoritism. I've always hated it," she said impatiently. This was another opportunity of a lifetime that circumstances were forcing her to turn her back on. She knew life was hard, but nobody had told her it was going to be this rough, she thought unhappily.

Nick took her hand and led her into the den. "You are screeching so loudly that your voice is going to crack the crystal," he said, his eyes indicating the chandelier that twinkled and sparkled overhead. "I don't want Bernice having heart failure in the morning," he said, referring to his housekeeper. Firmly, he shut the door of the den behind him. Nothing but the fireplace illuminated the room. "Now, you listen to me before you get on that high horse of yours. All I did was direct Alex's attention to you."

"You call sending a man airplane tickets directing his attention?" she asked incredulously.

"I call that being polite," he said. "First I had

Scottie go to the local library and get back issues of *Rendezvous* and make copies of your articles. Then I gave Alex a call, telling him about you and offering to forward the articles. I sent the tickets because I didn't want to inconvenience the man any further. It was *his* choice to come, *his* choice to offer you the job. Your merit got him to do that, not any magical powers of mine!"

The light of the fire bathed his face in hypnotic, warm hues. Shane reached out and ran her hand along the outline of his beard, her fingers tingling from the sensation. "Why did you do all that?" she asked.

"Because, milady, I'm a firm believer that husbands and wives should try to stay on the same side of the continent whenever possible. It makes the trip to the bedroom that much shorter," he told her, taking her into his arms.

"Husbands and wives?" she repeated, her heart hammering so hard she knew he must feel it too.

"Um-hmm. In case you've forgotten, I did ask you to marry me."

She raised her eyes to his. "I haven't forgotten. I just believed that you'd thought better of the idea," she said in a small voice.

"How could I have improved on the best idea I've ever had?"

"Then, you still want to marry me?" she asked, not able to believe it. Why her? Why did she deserve to be the lucky one, when millions of women adored him? *Millions*, her mind echoed.

"Still? Lady, I'd move heaven and earth to have you," he said, his hold on her tightening as he kissed her cheek, his lips trailing off to the side of her neck.

"Why?" she asked, her mind beginning to reel, the way it always did when he touched the sensitive areas of her body.

"Why?" He chuckled. "Ah, there is a bit of female vanity to you, isn't there?" he asked, pulling her down on his lap as he sank into the comfortable cushions of the sofa that faced the fireplace. "Because," he said, slowly beginning to unzip the back of her dress, "you're warm, vibrant, sensitive, intelligent, and you love me."

She felt the shoulders of the dress slip down. "Millions of women love you."

"Millions of women love the image of Nick Rutledge. You've proven you love the man. You've proven that you can stand being pulled out of bed at ridiculous hours, trudge manfully—womanfully?" he amended, raising a teasing eyebrow in her direction—"up a snow-encrusted hill to ski with me. Camp out with only a few whimpers, and even put up with near-drowning without immediately thinking of either suing me or blackmailing me." He nibbled on the soft outline of her breasts left uncovered by the top of her bra. Her dress now rested about her waist. She scarcely noticed.

"But I'll age," she said sadly.

"Most people do," he pointed out. "I intend to."

"That's one of nature's jokes." She thought of all the stories she had read about men leaving their wives for younger women. How much more susceptible to that sort of temptation Nick would be than the average male, she lamented, surrounded constantly by nubile beauties all vying for his favors. "Older men are still attractive. Older women are just—older."

Expertly, Nick unhooked her bra, slipping the delicate straps off her shoulders. "But I like older women," he said, leering at her. "Just wait and see how wild I'm going to be around you when you're ninety-six," he promised, snuggling up to her freed breasts.

Darts of excitement danced through her as she cradled his head, savoring the feel of his hair against her soft skin. For a moment, she was lost in the rapture that was swiftly overtaking her.

"So will you say yes already?" Nick asked, looking up at her.

"Yes already," Shane murmured, her heart singing.

"Good," Nick said, sliding her off his lap and onto the sofa. He slipped the dress the rest of the way down, discarding it on the floor. She lay before him, ready. "I hate a contrary woman," he said huskily, beginning to form a trail of kisses along her body that was meant to drive her beyond the brink of exhilaration, into a sea of joy.

And it did, bringing with it the promise of a tomorrow that would be even more wonderful than today; a tomorrow made wonderful by the continual joining of two irresistible forces.

"I love you, Nick," Shane whispered hoarsely.

"I sure in hell hope so," Nick said. His mouth moved to her ear, and he whispered, "Because I love you with all my heart, and soul . . . and body."

The flames from the fireplace flickered warmly on the outlines of their bodies as they merged into one.

# THE EDITOR'S CORNER

*Ti amo. Ich liebe dich. Je t'aime. I love you.* Those words along with all the other magical words in our LOVESWEPT romances are read by women around the world. We thought you'd be interested to learn that our books are translated into lots of languages for publication in many, many countries. So you share our delicious stories with women everywhere: Australia, Germany, France, New Zealand, Sweden, Norway, the Philippines . . . I could go on and on. And fan mail reaches us with the most exotic postmarks—Selangor, Malaysia, for example. Those postmarks certainly conjure romantic images for us on the LOVESWEPT staff. It is deeply touching to know that the tenderness, humor, warmth, sensuality—all the elements of loving in our LOVESWEPT romances—are enjoyed equally by the reader in Kansas City and in Kuala Lumpur. Close your eyes. Can you imagine the globe circled by women touching hands, sharing the common belief that stories about loving relationships are the best entertainment of all? It's a beautiful image, isn't it?

Now from the universal to the particular—namely, the treats in store for you next month.

Heading off the April LOVESWEPT list is Joan Domning's fourth romance, **KIRSTEN'S INHERITANCE,** LOVESWEPT #29. This absolutely heartwarming story is set in the tiny town of Avlum, Minnesota, and features the colorful and sexy hero, Dr. Cory Antonelli. The darling doctor rocks the town Kirsten has grown up in. (His jogging clothes appear to be underwear to the small town folks amazed by his activities in their midst.) And he is so darkly handsome in a town of fair people of Scandinavian heritage that not a single thing he does can escape notice. Author Joan knows of what she speaks! She was born and raised in a community

*(continued)*

quite similar to the imaginary one in which she sets this charming book. There are creative twists galore in this love story that I feel sure you're going to add to your collection of "keepers."

OOO-h, that Iris Johansen! Better read **RETURN TO SANTA FLORES**, LOVESWEPT #40, with great care! It's always a challenge to try to figure out which of Iris's secondary characters has his or her own love story next, isn't it? One hint: maybe the way to a woman's heart is *not* via the palate, but another sense. Now, though, let's focus on the marvelous romance between Steve and Jenny in **RETURN TO SANTA FLORES**. First, you'll notice that the opening chapter takes place eight years before chapter two. It's almost a prologue to the story and a delightful innovation in the writing craft for this particular romance. Steve considers himself years too old and jaded for Jenny . . . but she won't take "no" for an answer. Her scrapes and Steve's last minute rescues become legendary around the hotel he owns, but through everything the real question still remains: can Steve resist Jenny's love? There is a comic scene in a motel bedroom in this, Iris's eighth romance, that is priceless!

What a pleasure to be able to introduce yet another talented newcomer as a LOVESWEPT author. **THE SOPHISTICATED MOUNTAIN GAL**, LOVESWEPT #41, is Joan Bramsch's first novel. And it's a "WOW" of a love story. Crissy Brant is one of the most vivacious and wide-ranging heroines we've published. She is an Ozark Mountain gal, but she's also a sophisticated and well-trained actress with a unique ability to create characters in many different voices. James Prince, a disillusioned ad man recently transplanted to Bransom, Missouri, has started a new life as a toy manufacturer. He falls in love first with Crissy in her role of Tulip Bloom, the Silver Dollar City storyteller . . . and soon he's in love with all the other Crissy Brants, too. But outsiders don't win trust easily and James has several

strikes against him—so the path to true love for these two delightful characters is as hard to negotiate as a steep and stone-strewn mountain road. By the way, there is a twenty-plus page "temptation" scene in this book that I guarantee will knock your socks off! My, oh my! Welcome to LOVESWEPT, Joan Bramsch!

Sara Orwig's first LOVESWEPT, **AUTUMN FLAMES,** received wonderful fan mail! Now Sara's topped even that romance with **HEAT WAVE,** LOVESWEPT #42. Marilee O'Neil literally drops into Cole Chandler's lap. Imagine Cole's surprise when, while sunbathing nude, a hot air balloon piloted by Marilee plunks down in the middle of his swimming pool. She claims to lead a dull and ordinary life—and perhaps that was the case *before* she met Cole. But life is anything but ordinary around this extraordinary hero. From painting his house on his wheat farm, to tutoring his nephew, to single-handedly capturing two rustlers on his property, Marilee's existence simmers in Cole's company. It's the hottest summer Kansas has known in recorded history . . . but the weather is cool in comparison to the sizzling love affair between two touching human beings. Sara Orwig just gets better and better all the time!

It's a pleasure to work with all these fine LOVESWEPT authors and a pleasure to hear from you that you are enjoying the series so much!

Until next month, we send warmest good wishes,
Sincerely,

*Carolyn Nichols*

Carolyn Nichols
Editor
*LOVESWEPT*
Bantam Books, Inc.
666 Fifth Avenue
New York, NY 10103